RAIN OF DEATH

Touch the Sky fell silent, squinting at a spot on the cliff just below them. It was foolish, of course, but Touch the Sky could almost swear he had seen sparks fly from the face of the—

There! There it was again. Sparks.

Something tickled his left ear. More sparks flew into his eyes. And then, with a sinking feeling in his belly like a chunk of cold lead, he realized that arrows were pelting them! And the sparks were because these arrows were special Comanche arrows tipped with white man's sheet iron, not flint. Iron tips bent and clinched when they hit bone, making them much more deadly.

Touch the Sky had no time to wonder how the renegades had guessed their plan. A Comanche could launch a large handful of arrows in mere seconds, and the sheer number coming in now, obviously launched from the base of the cliff, turned the air deadly all around them.

Finally, the barrage slowed and seemed to stop. Touch the Sky, holding his next breath, finally began to expel it in relief. Suddenly, one final arrow found them. And Touch the Sky heard the sickening noise, like an ax cutting a side of meat, as the iron-tipped arrow sliced into Little Horse's calf.

The *Cheyenne* Series:

1: ARROW KEEPER
2: DEATH CHANT
3: RENEGADE JUSTICE
4: VISION QUEST
5: BLOOD ON THE PLAINS
6: COMANCHE RAID
7: COMANCHEROS
8: WAR PARTY
9: PATHFINDER
#10: BUFFALO HIDERS
#11: SPIRIT PATH
#12: MANKILLER
#13: WENDIGO MOUNTAIN
#14: DEATH CAMP
#15: RENEGADE NATION
#16: ORPHAN TRAIN
#17: VENGEANCE QUEST
#18: WARRIOR FURY
#19: BLOODY BONES CANYON

CHEYENNE

RENEGADE
SIEGE

JUDD COLE

LEISURE BOOKS   NEW YORK CITY

A LEISURE BOOK®

December 1996

Published by

Dorchester Publishing Co., Inc.
276 Fifth Avenue
New York, NY 10001

CHEYENNE #20:

RENEGADE SIEGE

Prologue

Although Matthew Hanchon bore the name given to him by his adopted white parents, he was the son of full-blooded Northern Cheyennes. The lone survivor of a bluecoat massacre in 1840, the infant was raised by John and Sarah Hanchon in the Wyoming Territory settlement of Bighorn Falls.

His adoptive parents loved him as their own, and at first, the youth was happy enough in his limited world. The occasional stares and threats from some white settlers meant little—until his sixteenth year brought a forbidden love for Kristen, daughter of the wealthy rancher Hiram Steele.

Steele's campaign to run Matthew off like a distempered wolf was assisted by Seth Carlson, a jealous, Indian-hating cavalry officer who was in love with Kristen. Carlson delivered a fateful ultimatum: Either Matthew cleared out of Bighorn Falls for good, or Carlson would break the Hanchons' contract to supply nearby Fort Bates, thus ruining their mercantile business.

His heart sad but determined, Matthew set out for the up-country of the Powder River, Cheyenne territory. Captured by braves from Chief Yellow Bear's tribe, the youth was declared an Indian spy for the hair-face soldiers. Matthew was brutally tortured over fire. Then, only a heartbeat before he was to be scalped and gutted, old Arrow Keeper interceded.

The tribe shaman and protector of the sacred Medicine Arrows, Arrow Keeper had recently experienced an epic vision. This vision foretold that the long-lost son of a great Cheyenne chieftain would return to his people and lead them in one last great victory against their enemies. This youth would be known by the distinctive mark of the warrior, the same birthmark Arrow Keeper spotted buried past this youth's hairline: a mulberry-colored arrowhead.

Arrow Keeper used his influence among the tribesmen to save the youth's life. He also ordered that Matthew be allowed to join the tribe and train with the junior warriors. This action especially infuriated two braves: the fierce war leader Black Elk and his cunning cousin Wolf Who Hunts Smiling.

Black Elk was jealous of the glances cast at the tall young stranger by Honey Eater, daughter of Chief Yellow Bear. And Wolf Who Hunts Smiling, proudly ambitious despite his youth, hated all whites without exception. This stranger, to him, was only a make-believe Cheyenne who wore white man's shoes, spoke the paleface tongue, and showed his emotions in his face like the woman-hearted white men.

To help Matthew become accepted by the tribe, Arrow Keeper buried his white name forever and gave him a new Cheyenne name: Touch the Sky. But the youth remained a white man's dog in the eyes of many in the tribe. At first humiliated at every turn, the determined youth eventually mastered the warrior arts. Slowly, as his coup stick filled with enemy scalps, he won the respect of more and more of his people.

Touch the Sky helped save his village from Pawnee attacks. He defeated ruthless whiskey traders bent on destroying the Indian way of life. He outwitted land-grabbers intent on stealing the Cheyenne homelands for a wagon road. He saved Cheyenne prisoners kidnapped by Kiowas and Comanches during a buffalo hunt. He rode north into the Bear Paw Mountains to save Chief Shoots Left Handed's Cheyennes from Seth Carlson's Indian-fighting regiment. He ascended fearsome Wendigo Mountain to recover the stolen Medicine Arrows. And he saved Honey Eater and many others when he risked his life to obtain a vaccine against the deadly Mountain Fever.

But with each victory, deceiving appearances triumphed over reality, and the acceptance Touch the Sky so desperately craved eluded him. Worse yet, his hard-won victories left him with two especially fierce enemies outside the tribe: a Blackfoot called Sis-ki-dee and a Comanche named Big Tree.

As for the Cheyenne warrior Black Elk, he was hard but fair at first. When Touch the Sky rode off to save his white parents from outlaws, however, Honey Eater was convinced that Touch the

Sky had deserted her and the tribe forever. She was forced to accept Black Elk's bride-price after her father crossed to the Land of Ghosts. But Touch the Sky returned.

Then, as it became clear to all that Honey Eater loved Touch the Sky only, Black Elk's jealousy drove him to join his younger cousin in plotting against Touch the Sky's life. Finally, Wolf Who Hunts Smiling's treachery forced a crisis: Aiming at Touch the Sky in heavy fog, he instead killed Black Elk. Now Touch the Sky stands accused of the murder in the eyes of many.

Though their love divided the tribe irrevocably, Touch the Sky and Honey Eater performed the squaw-taking ceremony and now have a son. He has firm allies in his blood brother Little Horse, the youth Two Twists, and Tangle Hair. With Arrow Keeper's mysterious disappearance, Touch the Sky has become the tribe shaman. But an unholy alliance between Wolf Who Hunts Smiling, Big Tree, and Sis-ki-dee has given birth to the Renegade Nation. The Nation's chief goal is the destruction of Touch the Sky, who remains trapped between two worlds, welcome in neither.

Chapter One

"Brother," Touch the Sky called out, "come out and help me smoke this pipe."

All Cheyenne lodges were raised with their entrances facing east toward the sun and the source of all life. And now the elkskin entrance flap of Little Horse's tipi was thrown back, letting in the bright coppery sunshine. Sitting just inside the entrance on a heap of soft buffalo robes, the sturdy brave was polishing a beautiful silver dagger.

Little Horse knew from long acquaintance with Touch the Sky's tone and manner that the tall brave had not stopped by to discuss the causes of the wind. But custom dictated that warriors never come at an important subject too directly. So Little Horse stepped outside and joined his friend in the lush new grass that was already past their ankles.

Little Horse held his Spanish dagger out in the sunlight, and the brilliant reflection made Touch the Sky squint. The blade was double-honed, fine-tempered steel, the haft pure silver inlaid with an exquisite ruby.

"Time is a bird, buck." Little Horse nodded at the dagger while Touch the Sky lit his clay calumet with a borrowed coal. "You gave me this as a gift when Honey Eater told you she was heavy with child. Now that child has two winters behind him and roars like a silvertip bear. Time is a bird, and the bird is on the wing."

Little Horse's words reminded Touch the Sky that their people were preparing for another uneasy season of their camp being divided against itself. It was early in the Moon When the Green Grass Is Up, and this Cheyenne band under the new chief named River of Winds had recently packed their entire camp onto travois. Facing east, singing the Song to the New Sun Rising, they rode out one morning at dawn from their winter home in the Tongue River Valley.

Their ponies were winter worn, gaunt from a scant diet of cottonwood bark, twigs, and buds. The first of the warm moons would be spent grazing the ponies at this permanent summer camp near the fork of the Powder and the Little Powder. Once the ponies had their strength again, herd scouts would be sent out to locate Uncle Pte, the buffalo. Then would come the annual hunt.

All that was normal, thought Touch the Sky, or so it might seem to the causal observer. But in truth death stalked this camp, watching for his chance like a cat on a rat.

For some time further, the two braves discussed inconsequential matters and kept a close eye on the activity around them. Finally, Touch the Sky laid the pipe down on the ground between them—the sign that serious discussion could begin.

"Look there." He gazed toward the vast central clearing.

Little Horse followed his friend's eyes. Beyond the youths wrestling in the clearing, past the first clan circles of tipis, stood the lone tipi of the brave named Medicine Flute. Only two Cheyennes were permitted, by custom, to live outside of the clan gatherings: the peace chief River of Winds, who had been voted peace leader after the brutal murder of Chief Gray Thunder, and the tribe's shaman, the title held—though under dispute—by Touch the Sky and claimed by Medicine Flute.

"What do you notice about the bone blower's lodge?" Touch the Sky asked. He had used the contemptuous name all in his band gave Medicine Flute, whose so-called flute was a crude instrument made from a human leg bone.

"Only this," Little Horse replied. "That it is quiet of late. Too quiet."

Satisfied, Touch the Sky pursed his lips into a grim straight line. He was at least a head taller than most braves in camp and muscled more like the Apaches to the southwest than like the typically slender-limbed Plains Indians. A strong hawk nose set off an intelligent face. He wore his black hair long, except where it was cut short over his eyes to clear his vision. His scarred chest and arms, pocked by burns and knife scars and old bullet wounds, told the violent history of his life among the red men.

"Too quiet indeed, buck. Your thoughts fly with mine. They should all be gathered there, should they not? All of our enemies within the tribe. Medicine Flute, Wolf Who Hunts Smiling, the Bull Whip soldiers. Gathered there and plotting."

"But they are not," Little Horse said, continuing his friend's line of thought. "Why?"

"Because they had all the time of the short white days to plot in our winter camp. And now they have their plan."

"And whatever it is," Little Horse said, glancing west toward the distant ranges of the Sans Arc Mountains, "has something to do with all the word-bringers they have sent to the renegades on Wendigo Mountain."

"Buck, I am called shaman, but you too see which way the wind sets." Touch the Sky gazed toward those distant peaks. Wendigo Mountain could not be seen from there because its tip was always enshrouded in steam that escaped from underground hot springs.

"Their disappointment was keen," Little Horse said, "when you returned from Bloody Bones Canyon up north. They were sure that Sis-ki-dee had sent you under."

"He did send me under," Touch the Sky said, recalling the huge rockslide Sis-ki-dee sent crashing down on him. "But the High Holy Ones did not choose to leave me there. Not only did I disappoint the Contrary Warrior, but you kept our enemies in camp from seizing the reins of power. All winter they have been seething, as frustrated as badgers in a barrel. Now they will come at us with a vengeance."

"But how?" Little Horse asked. "And where? I

see no preparations, no plotting, no gathering of weapons. The Bull Whips have not been working their ponies, and even more ominous, they have actually been civil toward the Bow String troopers, their sworn enemies. Yes, they seem to expect some great event. Yet they hardly seem prepared for it themselves."

"Brother, you have placed the ax on the helve," Touch the Sky agreed, and again his deep-set black eyes cut toward the Sans Arc range. "They expect trouble, but this time they will not be a part of it."

"They let Sis-ki-dee kill our last chief," he mused, avoiding Gray Thunder's name, as one did when speaking of the dead. "And I fear they are depending on him again. Him or Big Tree. Or even worse, both of them with their combined camp of murdering Kiowas and Comanches."

"A strike on our camp?" Little Horse said.

"Anything is possible. I will speak with Tangle Hair and Two Twists. Everyone in our little band must watch with the vigilance of five men. They are both on herd guard now. I will speak to them when they return."

"Speaking of trouble clouds blowing our way," Little Horse said, "look what approaches from the river."

Touch the Sky glanced down the long, sloping bank of grass that ended at the spring-swollen Powder. A small but powerfully built brave approached them at a cautious, oblique angle. His eyes constantly shifted, darted, watched for the ever expected attack.

"No need to take up weapons," Wolf Who Hunts Smiling called over, seeing the dagger glint in Little Horse's hand. "My weapons are back in my tipi."

Touch the Sky's lips curled back in a sneer. "Little Horse, do you smell sweet lavender? Honeyed words from a stinking, murdering snake?"

Little Horse nodded. "As you say. Look how he comes to council. He who has killed our own. He who has tried to kill your wife and babe and each of us in our turn. A worm who grins like a wolf and tries to look you in the eye like a man."

For a moment, Wolf Who Hunts Smiling almost lost honor by showing his rage. But he managed to hold his face impassive as a warrior should. Indeed, it was Touch the Sky's ignorant mistake of showing his feelings in his face—when he was first captured many winters ago—that had earned him the name Woman Face from his enemies.

"Never mind," Wolf Who Hunts Smiling said, still strangely calm, it seemed to both braves. Alarmingly so. This was the confident manner of a man who held the high ground and all the escape trails. "Never mind your blustering and insults. I have a destiny to fulfill and you two jays have irked me long enough. I admit you are both warriors and nothing else. Tangle Hair and young Two Twists also. Four bucks worth twenty, all worthy to wear the medicine hat into battle."

Neither brave said a word to this. Their impassive faces, however, disguised amazed minds. This conciliatory tone and these laudatory words were no part of the wily wolf they knew—unless he had a new plan.

"You are warriors," Wolf Who Hunts Smiling repeated. "I have been unable to kill you. Nor have you killed me, though both of you have tried more than once."

"And will again," Little Horse promised.

"Never mind all this praising of us," Touch the Sky said impatiently. "My boasts are made with weapons, and your praise I do not value at all. I have no ears for it. Crack the nut and expose the meat. I am sick of looking on your putrid, murdering form."

"Just this, Noble Red Man. I need fighters like you. Cross your lances over mine, swear allegiance to my new Renegade Nation, and we will enjoy equal shares of the plunder. Your band, united with mine, Sis-ki-dee's, and Big Tree's! Bucks, why push when a thing will not move? We cannot kill one another, and we are in each other's way. So why not instead profit together?"

"Listen to this jay," Touch the Sky said. "Setting himself up as a Roman Nose and turning us into his Dog Soldiers to slay the old headmen in their sleep. The bravery of the Spaniards and the whiskey traders."

"You have heard me. I will not repeat the offer. Know this. Certain events are even now being set in motion. The outcome of these events will enrich my Renegade Nation beyond any peyote fantasy. Once these riches are mine, I will not need you and your followers. The renegades will be armed with the new paleface repeaters and lavishly equipped for battle."

Wolf Who Hunts Smiling suddenly spat, his gesture showing a glimpse of his usual manner around his enemies. "You can ride with me or continue fighting me. But if you cannot stop us now, how will you when we are stronger than a bluecoat regiment?"

This question, Touch the Sky realized, explained Wolf Who Hunts Smiling's new confidence. The murderous brave and his allies were about to strike at some wealthy hair-face interest, and the thought did indeed alarm Touch the Sky. Wolf Who Hunts Smiling had explained matters with a cold accuracy. Since so many blue-bloused soldiers had been called back beyond the Great Waters, possibly to fight their own white brothers, few soldiers remained.

If the Renegade Nation obtained such equipment as Wolf Who Hunts Smiling boasted of, Touch the Sky knew they would control the West. The fierce Blackfeet warriors to the north had been wiped out by the yellow vomit, and the Crow Nation was unmanned by strong water. No one could stop them.

"At least tell us this fine plan," Touch the Sky replied. "I already know of worse treachery involving you. Why hesitate to say which whites you are attacking? It cannot be my parents this time. They don't have the riches you boast of. So why not tell us like a man instead of hinting like the girls in their sewing lodge?"

Wolf Who Hunts Smiling flashed a cunning grin. "Good attempt, buck, but I will not tell you. Just count upon it. The worm will turn and soon. For the sake of your wife and child, if nothing else, consider my offer."

With those ominous words, Wolf Who Hunts Smiling turned and walked back toward the common clearing. Baffled and worried, Little Horse and Touch the Sky exchanged a long look. And his enemy's veiled words sparked in Touch the Sky's thoughts like burning twigs: *Certain events are even now being set in motion.*

*   *   *

"Last spelling lesson, we talked about mnemonic tricks," Kristen Steele said. "Faith, what do I mean by mnemonic?"

Faith Gillycuddy, one of the brightest pupils in the sixth form, stood up from the long wooden bench where she sat with the rest of the older girls. "It's from the Greek word for memory, and the first m is silent. A mnemonic device is a trick to aid your memory."

Kristen nodded. Tall and willow slender, she was in her early twenties. Her hair was as golden as new oats, and her cornflower-blue eyes were as bottomless as a cloudless sky. "Such as?"

"There's a rat in the word separate. That reminds you not to place an e in the middle of the word."

Kristen started to speak, then caught herself and waited for the big steam auger to quit its grinding roar. Teaching in a mine-camp school had definite advantages. Chief among them was the fact that the kids could not easily play hooky since they lived too close to school. But fighting to be heard above the blasts, digging, and constant mucking of ore made her feel like a sergeant, not a teacher.

"Very good," Kristen said when she could be heard. "On the last spelling test, nearly all of you misspelled the word dessert. You confused it with the word desert. Rather than copying the words over and over in your hornbooks, we can make up a mnemonic device. Just remember that dessert is something sweet."

"Aw, hell, Miz Steele," piped up Justin McKinney, son of the mine foreman. "Now you got my stomach growlin'."

19

"For swearing in the classroom," Kristen said sternly to check the other students' laughter, "you'll stay after school for one hour and split stove lengths."

"Aw, hell! You're a nice lady and all, but who cares about any ol' stupid spelling rules?" Justin demanded. "I'm gonna be a miner like my old man and his old man before him. My pa can't even sign his name, and he runs this gang—after Mr. Riley, of course. If pa can't cipher or write, why should I?"

Despite his spirited mouth, Justin had a good nature and what Kristen termed a rude sense of honor. His occasional rebellions in class did not usually bother her. Now, as she glanced out the little room's only sash window at the tidy streets of the Far West Mining Camp, she resisted an affectionate smile. For the sake of discipline, she must maintain her dignity.

"For your information, young man, it was your father who first suggested this school to Caleb Riley."

"He did?" Justin looked betrayed and embarrassed.

"He most certainly did. And he told me that he hoped I could make something out of his boy besides a hardheaded, cussing worker. He wants you to be a mining engineer, not just a gang boss."

"Well, I'll be dam—uh—darned," Justin said.

"He also told me," Kristen added, fighting hard to quell her mirth, "that if I had any trouble from you I should just remind you of the cowhide strop hanging on the door at home."

Justin turned pale and quickly opened his hornbook. "Dessert is something sweet," he repeated as he hastily wrote, and the rest of the class laughed again. This time Kristen joined them.

Taking a chance while the teacher was in a good mood, Sarah Blackford raised her hand.

"Yes, Sarah?"

"Miss Steele, is it true that you're going to marry Caleb Riley's brother Tom, the officer from Fort Bates?"

All of the students stared eagerly at Kristen, and she felt the color come into her face. "We are at our lessons right now, not larking about on Fiddler's Green!"

"She's gettin' married!" Justin exclaimed. "Look at her flush!"

Suddenly, anger warmed Kristen's face. But even as she opened her mouth to reprimand her students, an explosion of gunfire rose above the steady din of the mines.

After an instant of frozen shock, Kristen ran to the propped-open plank door and peered outside. The mining camp was established in a tea-cup-shaped hollow about halfway up a mountain. The schoolhouse was centered among the few streets of simple but sturdy houses made with raw planks and shake roofs. The other half of the hollow was taken up by the mining operation itself.

The entire camp was encircled by a high ridge. Kristen glanced upward and felt her stomach turn to ice when she saw that the entire ridge was covered with armed Indian warriors, their faces garish with battle paint.

A teamster was hauling a wagon of ore toward the railroad siding, where a steam locomotive hooked to several long wagons waited on the spur line. Touch the Sky had sighted that railroad through the mountains for Caleb. The warriors' assistance in building the vital rail link to Register Cliffs had made this mining operation possible. Now, as Kristen watched in horror, the teamster rolled sideways off his wagon, one side of his face a red smear.

Arrows were flying in so heavily that the air was blurred from them. Benny Havens, the camp courier, caught one in the neck and crumpled to his knees. Up near the head frame of the mine, a man emptying a slusher bucket suddenly collapsed and rolled down into the camp, bouncing hard off the rock-strewn slope.

A woman was returning from the company mercantile with a basket of goods. It was Tilly Blackford, Sarah's mother. Kristen cried out when the woman's white bodice suddenly erupted with a scarlet stain before she collapsed.

"No!" Kristen shouted when a few of the boys leapt forward to see what was happening. "Down! Everyone, get down on the floor. It's an Indian attack!"

This news immediately prompted a chorus of screams from the girls, and even the boys turned pale. However, no one obeyed the teacher until a bullet shattered the only window and sent shards of glass flying in like tiny spears.

Chapter Two

"Have ears, Quohada!" said Sis-ki-dee, known as the Contrary Warrior among his few friends and the Red Peril among his many enemies.

The huge Quohada Comanche named Big Tree turned his grinning face from the sight below to listen. Both renegades were flushed with triumph as they watched the miners scurrying around, dousing fires, and tending to their wounded and dead.

"It was a good first strike," Sis-ki-dee said. "We have not lost a man, yet they have lost several. And only look."

He pointed to two mobile wagons loaded with equipment for the Beardslee Flying Telegraph, a portable telegraph capable of sending sonic codes short distances without copper wires and insulators. Both wagons still burned.

"Now they cannot send words through the air

to Register Cliffs. Our men have already torn out the rails of the path for their iron horse. So they can neither escape nor receive any supplies. We have them under siege. With our position here on this excellent high ground, we will make their world a hurting place!"

Sis-ki-dee flashed his crazy grin. He sat on a big claybank atop the long curving ridge that surrounded the mining camp. Big brass rings dangled from slits in his ears, and heavy copper brassards protected his upper arms from enemy lances and axes. His face, once ruggedly handsome, was badly marred by smallpox scars. In defiance of the long-haired Blackfoot tribe that had banished him, he and all of his braves wore their hair cropped ragged and short. He had just finished sliding his .44-caliber North & Savage rifle into its buckskin sheath.

"We have them," Big Tree agreed. "And Wolf Who Hunts Smiling was right this time. We would lose too many men in a direct attack and might fail to take them. However, we can destroy them with a siege. We have them between the sap and the bark. They cannot leave or call for help nor can they receive supplies."

"Spoken straight arrow," Sis-ki-dee assured him. "And while we have them trapped, we turn the very Wendigo himself loose upon them! By night our fire arrows will warm the cool air; by day our bullets will hum around their ears like blowflies."

This was all true enough. But Big Tree smiled slyly, watching his companion from caged eyes. The Comanche's face was homely, characteristic of his tribesmen, who were considered the ugliest Indians on the plains—and the best horsemen on earth. An eagle-bone whistle hung around his neck, and a gaudy Presidential Medal was pinned to his rawhide shirt. This bore a likeness of the Great White Father and was one of those that had been presented to the tribes upon the most recent treaty signing—a treaty the hair faces violated before the ink was dry.

"Yes," Big Tree said, "we have them. But, of course, word will travel. And the tall bear caller will soon know that we have his friend Caleb Riley up against it. And that sun-haired beauty your loins ache for—the tall one once held her in his blanket for love talk! He will be here, Sis-ki-dee."

Fury burned in Sis-ki-dee's eyes, and at first, he said nothing. Big Tree was goading him, albeit indirectly because, once again, the tall Cheyenne warrior had eluded Sis-ki-dee's best efforts to kill him.

After murdering the Cheyenne Chief Gray Thunder, Sis-ki-dee had fled all the way north to dreaded Bloody Bones Canyon, his former stronghold in the Bear Paw Country. He knew Touch the Sky would follow him, and he had sworn to Big Tree, Wolf Who Hunts Smiling, and all of their followers that he would dangle the tall one's scalp from his sash. Instead, Sis-ki-dee had ended up humiliated and beaten.

But Sis-ki-dee brooked such treatment from no man. "Yes, he will come. And he will bring trouble when he does. But though I have failed to kill him, Quohada, he has not killed me."

"Not for lack of trying, Contrary Warrior. And how many times has he tried to make my wives widows?"

Sis-ki-dee watched the desperate activities below in camp and said, "As you say. So let him come. I am keen for sport. He will not stop us. He cannot. We two have both traded with the Comancheros in our Southwest homeland. We two know, Big Tree, what the red men here in the north country are only beginning to grasp. The whites place foolish value on the yellow rocks they dig from the ground."

He nodded toward the camp. "The yellow dust below will buy our men more new repeating rifles, more bullets, good white man's liquor and coffee, new scarlet strouding. And once we have wiped them out, their campsite will become our second stronghold, a hidden corral for our herds. With sentinels on these ridges, we would control the Sans Arcs Mountains."

Big Tree thrust his red-streamered lance out, and Sis-ki-dee crossed his lance over it. "From where we sit now to the place where the sun goes down," Big Tree vowed, "our enemies have no place to hide! This place hears me! This camp and everything in it is ours. And any man who means to stop us, white or red, will soon be feeding worms!"

Caleb Riley was a big-framed man presently dressed in buckskin trousers and shirt. Usually he also wore a broad-brimmed plainsman's hat and knee-length elkskin moccasins. But this morning, he had gone into the stopes to run a plumb line down a new shaft; so he had donned his heavy boots and a miner's helmet with a squat candle mounted in a little wire cage. He was still wearing them when the surprise attack began.

"Looks as if they're done tossing lead at us for now," Liam McKinney reported.

The burly foreman and his boss had taken cover behind a pile of shoring timbers. Now both men carefully searched the ridges above them.

"Damn featherheads," Liam added. "They shot down Jed Blackford's wife Tilly. Left him a widower and their girl Sarah half orphaned."

"That's just the beginning of our troubles, old son," Caleb said. The mine owner was still shy of 30, and he sported a full blond beard.

"What? Think they ain't done with us yet?"

Caleb shook his head. "I know they're not."

Liam's big bluff face was divided by a frown. "How can you know it, boss? I don't see one Injun up there now."

"When you can't see them," Caleb said, "is when you start worrying. My brother Tom has been fighting Indians since the Fort Laramie Accords started falling apart. Most tribes up here fight skirmish style. They hate to fort up, like white men. They take a shot at you from behind a rock, then move on to a new rock. They use very little organization or battle tactics. Instead, they rely on individual courage to inspire the rest and turn the battle."

Caleb nodded up toward the distant ridge. "But look here. These are Kiowas and Comanches, that renegade bunch from Wendigo Mountain. They'll turn a white man's tactics against him. And right now, my friend, they have us under siege."

"Siege?" Liam said doubtfully.

"Sure. Look at the Beardslee—first thing they burned. That was planned. Now we can't get word out. Want to wager they've taken up the tracks too at some point between here and Register Cliffs?"

27

Liam looked positively sick. "What in the hell for? What do a bunch of gut-eating savages want with this place?"

Caleb was so worried that his blond brows touched as the furrow between his eyes deepened in a frown. "Touch the Sky told me something a while back. He told me that the Comanches and Kiowas have learned the value of gold dust."

"Why even so, we don't have dust on hand! Hell, all we do is send out the ore to be mercury smelted! Those rocks are laced with color, but they're useless right now."

"They don't know we don't have dust on hand. They've learned the value of gold, but not how it's produced."

"Damn!" Liam exclaimed. "And you think they're layin' for us up there?"

Caleb didn't need to answer. At that moment, a miner broke cover and raced from the shelter of a pile of rocks toward his house and frightened family. He made it, but not without drawing several rifle shots and a flurry of arrows from above.

"Are you convinced?" Caleb asked grimly.

Liam swore quietly. "What do we do?"

"We've got men, and we've got arms," Caleb said. "Trouble is, we've also got one lousy position. Damn it, Liam! I've always meant to start posting a permanent guard up on that ridge. Touch the Sky suggested it almost a year ago. I've been so damn busy with these new stopes and recruiting men that I never got around to it."

Caleb swore again. "Well, they've got us! All these women and children. Anyway, we've got to take control. The only way to break a siege is to slip around them. We've got to somehow get word to my brother at Fort Bates. It's two days' hard ride southeast of here."

"What about Touch the Sky?" Liam suggested. "That red son can do for any grizz ever made, and that band of his is all grit and a yard wide."

"I won't send for him," Caleb decided. "He's put his ass on the line for us too much as it is. Besides that, we won't need to send for him. Nothing goes on around here that he doesn't hear about. We may be seeing him yet." Turning from Liam, Caleb called out, "Dakota!"

"Yo!" a voice answered from somewhere behind the mess tent.

"How's that little chestnut mare of yours?"

"Well grained and rested, boss. What's on the spit?"

"Come around to the office after sundown, and I'll tell you. I want you to run a message for me."

Then Caleb peered cautiously around the corner of the timbers. "Meantime, Liam, we've got to make plans for the defense of this camp. Either we roll up our sleeves and quick, or we're going to lose far more than our shirts. Liam, you know all the men by name better than I do. Draw up a list and divide them into three—no, four guard shifts. Six hours each stint, round the clock.

"Post men at the safest possible points among the houses and near the front entrance to camp. And get the order to all the houses: No one shows his face outside the houses by day until those Indians are cleared out. We've got one damned good woman to bury now. I don't want more. Just cross your fingers that we get a message through to Tom. If not, we'll soon be doing the hurt dance."

Chapter Three

Certain events are even now being set in motion.

Wolf Who Hunts Smiling's ominous promise stayed with Touch the Sky like a cankering sore, nagging at him even when he tried to ignore it.

In camp, the routine went forward, reassuring in its familiarity. Every few days, a hunting party rode out. For the time being, the game was plentiful again on the hunting ranges and near the salt licks. Other braves rode herd guard, tended the crude beaver traps, or formed scouting parties. These last were necessary to keep an eye on the movements of nearby red enemies such as the Crows to the north and the Pawnees to the east. Even more fearsome, however, was the new paleface militia called the Regulators. Now and then, Indian fever struck them, and they rode out to massacre a hunting party or terrorize a camp.

"Enough enemies already surround us," Two

Twists complained one night as he and Tangle Hair and Little Horse visited at Touch the Sky's lodge. "Yet we are forced to live like intruders in our own camp."

He nodded toward the buckskin Touch the Sky and Honey Eater had sewn to the inside of their tipi's thinning cover. Similar to the white man's wainscoting, it kept their shadows from showing in the firelight at night.

"You would talk of intruders to Touch the Sky?" Little Horse demanded. "He who has never known a day's true acceptance since he was first captured and brought in among us?"

Tangle Hair was playing with the rambunctious Little Bear, who was trying mightily to grab the strips of red-painted rawhide binding Tangle Hair's braid. The little one possessed amazing strength already. He was the pride of not only Touch the Sky and Honey Eater, but every brave in Touch the Sky's little band of followers. To an Indian, every adult in camp was parent to every child.

"No, I have never been accepted," their shaman said. "But I married the prettiest woman in this camp, and she gave me the finest son. Who are my companions? Only the best warrior between the Sweetwater and the Marias! Never mind singing a dirge for me. I have a more immediate question, bucks. Who knows why the Shoshone sent up smoke this day?"

The Shoshone, with whom the Cheyennes had a shaky peace, lived to the northwest. They were the nearest tribe to the Sans Arcs, as every brave there realized. Pausing as she steeped yarrow tea for them, Honey Eater watched all of them with great interest. She would not speak up, of course,

31

in the presence of a group of men. These matters did not concern women. But she knew full well who lived in the Sans Arcs.

"You saw their smoke too?" Little Horse said. "I cannot read their sign. But I fear the worst trouble in the world will be found there since the messages went on all during the day."

Touch the Sky nodded. "As you say. Our Sioux cousins read their sign better. Perhaps soon we will see one and can ask."

He avoided Honey Eater's curious eyes. Not only did his worst enemies range the Sans Arcs, but the white woman he had once loved lived at the mining camp there. And she would realize he was worried about her.

"Not just the smoke," Little Horse said. "Do you hear them even now? The Bull Whips, I mean. Their lodge is a merry place this night. They are celebrating something. Not one of them does not smile cunningly at me. Something has happened, and they are very pleased, whatever it is."

"I have even heard some of them," Tangle Hair put in, "claim that they will attend the Renewal of the Arrows even though you are our shaman. Such talk worries me. They only cooperate when they have treachery planned or feel confident that we are entering the belly of the beast."

Despite the great dissension in the camp, the mighty Arrow Keeper had left the mantle of shaman on Touch the Sky's shoulders. Dutifully, he conducted the spiritual ceremonies in accordance with the Cheyenne Way handed down by the High Holy Ones. And before the next sunrise, he would cleanse the Arrows, a symbolic purging of the people's guilt and sins. The four sacred

Medicine Arrows were the center of their metaphysics, and it was his task as shaman and Keeper of the Arrows to keep them forever sweet and clean.

"Never mind them," Touch the Sky said. "Let them come or let them gather around Medicine Flute like flies on dung. I am indifferent. Our allies will be there, and we will renew the Arrows. And timely done, bucks! We will need all the strength and guidance of the Arrows if those smoke signals are as important as I fear they are."

Late the next day, while young women kept time with stone-filled gourds, many in the Powder River camp danced at the Renewal of the Arrows. Touch the Sky's clay-painted face was gruesome yet magnificent in the wavering glow of a huge ceremonial fire. This was a rite for the entire tribe, not just the warriors. All who were old enough soon circled the fire. Their knees kicked high as the hypnotic rhythm of stones and the regular cadence of "Hi-ya, hi-ya" lulled them and put the trance glaze over their eyes.

Not everyone came to support the ancient law ways. Touch the Sky could see the rebels, most of them Bull Whips loyal to Wolf Who Hunts Smiling, gathered around Medicine Flute's tipi. The false shaman was conducting the black-magic ceremony known as Praying A Man Into The Ground, and Touch the Sky knew that he was the man whose death they prayed for.

Touch the Sky's face was painted as for war: forehead yellow, nose red, chin black. He wore his single-horned warbonnet, its tail long with coup feathers. For a moment, Touch the Sky thought of the missing Arrow Keeper. And again he felt the power of his epic vision at Medicine Lake many winters ago—the vision quest Arrow Keeper had decreed so that the young warrior could learn his destiny.

Again those vivid and ominous images were laid over his eyes. Red men, thousands of them from every tribe west of the river called Great Waters, all danced as one people, expressing their misery, fear, and utter hopelessness. And on the horizon behind them, guidons snapping in the wind, sabers gleaming in the bloodred sun, came hordes of blue-bloused soldiers. But that vision gave way to more immediate trouble. Again the worried brave thought of all the smoke signals from the Sans Arcs.

Touch the Sky held the four sacred Arrows in a coyote-fur pouch. After the dancing, he unwrapped them and laid them on a stump in the center of camp. The shafts were striped blue and yellow, the crow-feather fletching was dyed bright red. With the Arrows thus presented, the people lined up to leave their gifts.

One by one, every member of the tribe with more than 12 winters behind him knelt beside the Arrows and left something. The gifts reflected their ability to give. Some left valuable pelts, rich tobacco, even weapons; the poorest among them left dyed feathers, decorated coup sticks, or moccasins with beaded soles.

After the gifts had been left, Touch the Sky recited the sacred Renewal Prayer in his most powerful voice. The words drowned out Medicine Flute's reedy voice and idolatrous murmurings.

Oh, Great Spirit of Maiyun,
whose voice we hear in the winds
and whose breath gives life to all the world,
hear us! We are small and weak. We need
your strength and wisdom.

"Let this be so," the people said as one.

Let us walk in beauty, and make our eyes ever
behold the red and purple sunset. Make our
hearts respect the things you have made and
our ears sharp to hear your voice. Make us
wise that we may understand the things you
have taught the people.

"Let this be so," the tribesmen repeated.

Let us learn the lessons you have hidden in
every leaf and rock.
We seek strength, not to be greater than our
brothers, but to fight our greatest enemy—
ourselves.
Make us always ready to come to you with
clean hands and straight eyes.

"Let this be so," the tribe sang as one.
Touch the Sky made a point of seeking the eyes
of Wolf Who Hunts Smiling. His voice swelled
with the power of a ferocious wind; so even his
enemies stood rooted as he concluded the Renewal Prayer in words that echoed out over the
campsite:

So when life fades, as the fading sunset,
our spirits may come to you
without shame.

Touch the Sky was staring dead at his enemy as he said the word shame. "Cheyenne people! The arrows have been renewed!"

Wolf Who Hunts Smiling and Medicine Flute only stared at him with mocking eyes. The only god, those looks promised, is the gun and the bullet. Our god will bury yours!

That night, as the clan fires began to bank, a Teton Sioux rode into camp. And after smoking to the directions with River of Winds, he told all of them what they had been waiting to hear, the reason for all those smoke signals of late. The renegades atop Wendigo Mountain had laid bloody siege to the whiteskin mining camp and clearly meant to annihilate them.

"This is fine news!" Wolf Who Hunts Smiling bellowed loud enough to be heard throughout the common clearing. "Of course, these renegades are our enemies. I lost two uncles at Wolf Creek, both scalped by Kiowas and Comanches raiding together as always. But no enemy is more dangerous than the hair faces! This one"—he pointed at Touch the Sky—"calls the miners his friend. He it was who sighted their path for the iron horse that daily crosses our ranges. He has sold our home to our enemies!"

"Odd," a Bow String soldier called out. "This mighty wolf rages about the miners, yet his stroud, his powder horn, and that steel knife in his sheath all came from the miners' peace price for using our land."

"Odd too," Two Twists said, "how the shifty wolf is so quick to assure us he hates the renegades. Odd, I say, since they are his blood brothers in treachery."

36

This remark incited an explosion of accusations and counteraccusations. River of Winds quickly interceded.

"We have a private treaty with the miners," the acting chief reminded all of his people, "voted for by the headmen. Only then did Touch the Sky sight their railroad for them. However, this new trouble is not our affair. These renegades are not on our homeland. It is pointless to start trouble in camp now. We are staying away from this fight."

This news clearly heartened the Bull Whips and took the fight out of them. As much as Touch the Sky respected River of Winds, he knew the chief was wrong. It was their fight.

Soon after Sister Sun rose the next day, Touch the Sky called a hasty council of his loyal band. As usual when serious trouble was afoot, they met in the comparative safety of the common corral surrounded by their ponies.

"Brothers," he told them, "have ears. Many in this camp, even among our supporters, take joy in this attack on my paleface friends. But it means far more than the loss of our trade goods. Do you see why Wolf Who Hunts Smiling and his lickspittles are rejoicing?"

Little Horse nodded, his features grim. "It is as clear as a blood spoor in new snow. This is only the first part of the final trail. With the riches they gain from this raid, they will become the best fighting force in the Red Nation."

Touch the Sky agreed. "As you say, buck. Even if this were not so, I would join the fight in the Sans Arcs. Caleb Riley is my friend. So are many of the others there, including Hiram Steele's daughter. However, I would not ask my men to ride with me. These are personal matters.

"I do ask you to ride because the welfare of our tribe is the issue. And I am glad that is true, for I know all of you well. You would ride with me no matter what. I do not place your lives in danger for my friends merely, but for the people. Tangle Hair?"

"I have ears."

"And a stout heart, warrior! I will not leave my wife and child alone in this camp. Nor will I trust any but a man from my band to protect them from these cunning red devils surrounding them. Do you believe me when I tell you it is no feather-bed job to remain behind here?"

Tangle Hair nodded. "They will be protected at the value of my very life."

"You two," Touch the Sky told Little Horse and Two Twists. "Ready your battle rigs. Never mind trying to hide your actions. Nor will we seek sanction of council. We will defy our chief and know that we serve a higher law in doing so. Our enemies will spread the familiar rumor that we have gone off to fight for white men against the interests of our own. Let them speak their bent words. If that mining camp falls, I lose more than good friends. We lose more. This camp will be their next target."

Chapter Four

"Tom!" Corey Robinson called out. "Tom Riley!"

A young towheaded army captain stopped halfway across the cracked dirt of what passed for a parade field at Fort Bates, Department of Wyoming. A redhead working on the new commissary building waved a hammer at him.

"Corey! Hey, boy, does your mother know you're out?"

A smile creasing his sunburned face, the officer crossed quickly toward his friend with his hand extended for a grip.

"So you got the contract for this job?" Tom said. "Good. Now I know the damn thing will stand up for at least a year. Last carpenter we hired used shoddy nails."

Corey flashed his gap-toothed grin. "Where you been, hoss? I been working on this job for two weeks. Ain't seen hide nor hair of you."

"Yeah, nobody has. You heard we have a new C.O.?"

Corey nodded. "Colonel Gilmer. I saw him once. Man looks like he's got a pinecone lodged up his sitter."

Tom glanced around. A working party led by a corporal marched past him, and he returned the corporal's salute.

"Corey, he's got bigger problems than a grouchy temper. We had a courier here last week, a civilian scout from Fort Dakota. He told me a few things. This Gilmer is tight with the Indian Ring back in Washington."

"Oh, no," Corey muttered. "Another one?"

Tom nodded. "He's been sent out here because, evidently, their graft and stealing got so blatant that somebody filed a complaint. And that's why you haven't seen me leading my platoon lately. Gilmer has assigned me to mapping-and-topog detail until further notice."

"What the hell's that?" Corey demanded.

"Mainly it's to get me out of the way. Guess who put him up to it?"

"Seth Carlson?"

"Seth Carlson. A man who parades himself as an army officer but who is, in fact, crooked as they come. So now I wander all over filling in terrain details on training maps of the area. Coffee-cooling detail."

Corey frowned. "Why get you out of the way all of a sudden?"

"That's what I was puzzling out when you called to me. If Carlson simply wanted to make my life miserable—a favorite pastime of his— then why stick me on such easy duty? The point was to keep me well away from the fort and especially from my men. I'm only back here now to resupply."

"I'll bet you a dollar to a doughnut," Corey said slowly, "that egg-sucking varmint Carlson is in cahoots with them renegades again. And that damned Wolf Who Hunts Smiling. Matthew is in for six sorts of hell, I'll bet."

"Not against me you won't bet," Tom assured him, "because my stick floats the same way as yours. If Carlson—"

"Sir! There you are, Cap'n. I've looked all over for you, sir."

A private with his loops unbuttoned, one of the new recruits sent to Fort Bates without previous training, saluted awkwardly.

"Salute with your right hand, trooper," Riley snapped.

"Uh, sorry, sir. This come for you by civilian messenger, sir. 'Bout two hours ago. I'm company runner, and he left it at headquarters. He was wantin' to see you really bad, but couldn't nobody find you."

"No," Riley said, his eyes meeting Corey's as he took the message. "I'm hard to find these days. Dismissed, Private."

He unfolded the sheet of foolscap and recognized his brother's handwriting immediately.

Tom: we're under siege by Kiowas and Co-manches from Wendigo Mountain. They've got us surrounded on the high ground. Tele-graph out; tracks ripped up. We mean to fight, but they seem dug in for the duration. Our supply line is cut. I don't know how long we can hold out. They're dealing us misery, big brother. We could sure use soldier blue right about now.

41

Corey had swung around to read the note over Tom's shoulder. Now both men locked gazes.

"Carlson knew," Tom seethed. "He knew! Damn his West Point bones! And Gilmer is no doubt in on it with him. It's useless to take this to Gilmer. Caleb's mine camp is just out of our jurisdiction anyway."

"Man alive," Corey said. "That bunch under Big Tree and Sis-ki-dee are the worst red trash on the plains. Kristen is up there."

Riley was already well aware of that fact. It was the main reason he had made so many trips up that way in the past few months.

Corey thought of something else. "Matthew will get sucked into this too."

Riley pushed his black-brimmed officer's hat back farther on his crown. His eyes cut to the quartermaster's office in a nearby whitewashed adobe building.

"Yeah," he said. "Matthew will get sucked into it. And I'm going to the fandango too. But not empty-handed if I can help it."

"I don't know, Tom," Oliver Dunbar said, cupping his goateed chin in one hand and rubbing it thoughtfully. "If we were still under Colonel Thompson, why, I'd do it. But this new C.O.—I don't know him yet. I won't take chances with an unknown quantity. I hear that Gilmer is the type to glance the other way if you catch my drift. But the thing of it is, he's new. A new commander sometimes has to lop off a few heads to establish his place in the pecking order. I'd rather not take any chances until I know which way the wind sets."

Riley frowned impatiently. "Well, I said I'd give you that mare of mine you're so sweet on. And I'll also toss in these."

The two officers sat in Dunbar's small cubbyhole office at the front of the supply building. Riley dipped one hand into his blue kersey trousers and removed a bunch of hard-times tokens—private coins issued by local businesses in nearby Bighorn Falls to combat the nation's critical shortage of specie. Soldiers used them as markers in poker games.

"All your markers," Riley told him, dropping them onto the top of the oak desk. "Almost fifty dollars' worth."

Dunbar's eyes widened and again he rubbed his chin. Clearly the quartermaster was tempted. "I don't know," he said slowly.

Now Riley played his ace. He bent down and unbuckled the beautiful star-roweled spurs that were the envy of every officer on post. He tossed them on the desk.

"Just to sweeten the pot, Ollie."

This offer weakened the last of Dunbar's resistance. He scooped the spurs and the poker markers into the wide top drawer of his desk.

"All right. I'll issue one Parrot muzzle loader. And ten rockets for it. But, Tom, you know damn well a cavalry officer has no legitimate right requisitioning an artillery rifle. So you best have a story made up in case someone decides to investigate."

"Never mind a story," Riley said. "Artillery won the war with Mexico and it's the future of warfare. If I'm questioned, I'll just say I want my platoon up to full capability."

"As for demolitions," Dunbar said, "all I have

43

on hand are a few one-pound blocks of nitro-glycerin. It's pure nitro oil, very volatile. It's been somewhat stabalized by adding an absorbent called kieselguhr so that it can be handled and transported. But it's still quite touchy—a sharp blow can set them off. Do you know the stuff?"

"No."

"I'll show you how to crimp the fuse and blast-ing cap to it. The main thing you have to watch is the fuse. The black powder in it gets dry out here. It's supposed to burn between thirty and forty-five seconds per foot, but you actually need to cut off a piece and burn it to find out the true rate."

Dunbar stared at Riley. "What the hell you got in mind, Tom?"

Riley was already rising from his chair. "Never mind. The less you know, the safer you are. C'mon. We're burning daylight. Show me how to prepare this nitro and let me sign the requisition. I've got to git and quick."

One day after Tom Riley set off for the north-west with a sturdy packhorse tied to his saddle horn by a lead line, his brother Caleb was still supervising the building of key defenses in his camp.

Working under cover of darkness, though rounds pinged in all through each night now, the miners evacuated the most vulnerable houses. These residents doubled up with those whose houses were less exposed to fire from the sur-rounding ridge.

The occupied houses were reinforced as much as possible. Boards were nailed over the win-dows, and water barrels were filled and set near

Renegade Siege

the corners in case of attack by fire arrows. To discourage any mounted attack in force, they set up pointed stakes at the two vulnerable approaches to the main camp. Caleb and Liam had also supervised the building of breastworks and rifle pits, and now the men were distributed better and under some cover, though still vulnerable to the high-ground marksmen.

Caleb's own house was too vulnerable; so his Crow Indian wife Woman Dress moved in temporarily with Kristen. Her own place, though uncomfortably accessible from above to lone intruders, was sheltered under pine trees and made for a poor rifle target.

"Nobody killed in the past twenty-four hours," Caleb informed both of them, having stopped by Kristen's place briefly to check on them and grab a quick cup of strong cowboy coffee. Kristen kept a pot going night and day now, as did many other women. They also had a plentiful supply of hot biscuits. The men, all standing guard in shifts, had little time for the luxury of meals.

Caleb looked exhausted. He hadn't been out of his clothes in more than two days, nor had he slept more than a few minutes at a time since the siege began.

"Any word of help?" Kristen asked.

Caleb shook his head. "I sent Dakota Boggs with a message for Tom. Dakota got through to the fort all right, but Tom wasn't there. Nobody would tell him where he is either, and they threw him off the post under threat of arrest. He was able to leave my note though. I just hope to God Tom gets it in time. If not—"

Caleb glanced at his wife and Kristen, then stopped before he said anything else about their

45

grim situation. Although her English was halting, Woman Dress understood his tone, and Caleb saw the fear stamped into her pretty features. Her fear wasn't for herself, but for her husband and the unborn child growing in her womb.

"We're strong right now," he amended, letting some light into this dark situation. "Down here, I mean. They'd pay dearly if they tried to rush us."

Caleb didn't give voice to what Kristen suspected really troubled him: the fact that they were completely cut off from resupply. Some things they had in abundance: coffee, flour, sugar, and, thank God, bullets. But this camp included infants, children, and other expectant mothers besides Woman Dress. Fresh milk and vegetables and medicines had been brought in almost daily from Register Cliffs. Now that supply line was cut off.

They had wounded badly in need of a doctor and would surely have more. And though it was a less urgent trouble right now, every day this huge operation was shut down was an enormous cost to Caleb. It wouldn't take that much longer to ruin it completely.

Even while Kristen reflected on these things, a rifle shot split the stillness as a renegade sniped from the ridge. All three of them winced. Suddenly, that lone shot was followed by a barrage and shouting from men in the mining camp.

Caleb ran to the front door and yelled out to a man named Perkins, "What's going on? They decide to rush us?"

"Hell, boss! Two fools are tryin' to ride in to camp. One's a soldier and the other is an Injun flyin' a truce flag! But they're dog meat! They'll never get through the lead!"

Chapter Five

The Shaiyena were rich in good ponies this season, having chased down a magnificent herd of wild mustangs from the mountains north of Beaver Creek. Touch the Sky had five on his string back at camp, and he chose his favorite for this sure-to-be dangerous mission. Light tan with an ivory mane and tail, the sturdy mare was of the type the whites called palomino.

With the accusing eyes of many in camp trained on them, Touch the Sky, Little Horse, and Two Twists rode out with their rope riggings heavy from battle gear. However, they had been heartened when many of the elders began the off-key minor chant reserved for warriors riding off to battle. The band still had supporters in camp, even if many of them were too old to paint for war.

Touch the Sky had grown accustomed to suspicious glances from his enemies. But even Honey Eater, though she understood the gravity of the situation at the mining camp, had met his eyes with a searching glance. The people say, that glance told him, that the sun-haired white woman is a beauty, that her eyes spark to life every time she looks at you.

The three Cheyennes made good time on their well-grazed mounts. They rode behind the timbered ridges until they left the tableland; then they struck out across the rolling brown plains after they forded the Bighorn River. Still almost a half day's ride southeast of the Sans Arcs range, they encountered a lone rider, who turned out to be Tom Riley.

The Cheyennes welcomed their friend with hearty bear hugs and thumps. The news that the white man was cut off from his men disheartened Touch the Sky since Riley's platoon was made up of seasoned veterans of Western warfare. But the supplies on Tom's packhorse—especially that artillery rifle—made up for the loss of some of them. Touch the Sky had seen the deadly results of Parrot muzzle loaders after Seth Carlson's platoon wiped out a Blackfoot camp with them.

As they neared the mountains, the flat land began to undulate into the foothills. While still well back from the miners, they began to hear the noises of sporadic shooting—sometimes an intense, sustained string of fire; other times lone, scattered shots.

"By God, Caleb is still fighting," Tom muttered.

Touch the Sky rode abreast him. Little Horse and Two Twists were on the flanks and a little behind, where they scanned the landscape for outlying Indian sentries.

"You expect anything but a fight from Caleb?" Touch the Sky said, the English words feeling odd and stiff in his mouth. It had been a long time since he used the language of his white parents.

"Hell, no! He's the one should've joined the army. Caleb's slow to rile, but once he rises on his hind legs, it's time to send for the undertaker."

Riley paused to backhand sweat from his brow. "But this isn't a fair fight, hombre. Those miners are plucky bastards—not a white liver among them. But they aren't the boys for a shooting war. Most of them never fired a real weapon, just squirrel pieces and such. And they don't know Indians, especially these Southwest Kiowas and Comanches. Worst of all, they're trapped on low ground and surrounded by an enemy on high ground. You don't have to sit on the benches at West Point to know that's trouble."

Touch the Sky nodded. "Speaking of high and low ground, do you know there's only one trail into the mining camp?"

It was Riley's turn to nod. "I wondered when we'd get around to that subject. Only one trail, you're saying, and that one covered by renegades."

"Covered as close as ugly on a buzzard. How do we ride in?"

"After dark?" Riley asked, then said, in answer to his own question, "Bad plan. We lose too much valuable time."

Touch the Sky threw a doubtful glance at Riley's big cavalry sorrel. Like most army horses, it was huge—seventeen hands high—and sleek from good grain. Such animals were strong, but out here in the wastes, they were also spoiled from pampered fort life.

"That animal know about bullets?" Touch the Sky asked.

Riley nodded. "Hates 'em. He's been in several skirmishes and always goes out of his way to duck them."

Touch the Sky nodded. "Good. You've seen how the red man rides when he's under fire. That's how we're going to ride in. Bold and right out in the open. You and I will split the flanks. Little Horse and Two Twists will ride behind us and cover the packhorse. A moving target is hard to hit. Just remember not to ride in a straight line for too long, or else they'll lead us and find their range."

"Brother!" Little Horse called over. "You two jays jabber on all day in the paleface tongue. What are you discussing?"

"Exactly how to get you killed," Touch the Sky called back.

"Good!" Little Horse, famous for his bravado when danger loomed, thumped his chest and let loose a war cry. "I have no plans to die in my tipi!"

At this bragging, Two Twists laughed outright. He stared across at Little Horse, who drew teasing lately because he had begun to grow a little stout. "No, you will not die in your tipi, All Behind Him, because by then you will not fit inside it!"

Little Horse glared back at the younger brave. "See? Take this brat away from his mother's dug and he becomes feisty!"

50

Bravado, however, was a paltry defense as the four riders drew near the troubled mountains. They were spotted well before they came into rifle range. From the ridges their enemy could see anyone approaching from the east.

"When you see the first dust puffs from their bullets," Touch the Sky called out to his companions, "touch up your ponies and fly like the wind!"

Soon, the first spiraling plumes of dust did begin to kick up all around them. The trail upward was wide to accommodate supply wagons and rutted from their passage. But the fleet, sure-footed mountain ponies bolted effortlessly as the Indians kicked them to a gallop. Riley's cavalry horse was only a bit slower and a tad less agile. The gelding was indeed bulletwise, and it wanted only to reach shelter.

Touch the Sky and his companions slid forward in the classic defensive riding position invented by the Cheyennes: They fell to one side of the pony's neck, hanging on for dear life and pulling their bodies low behind the horse's bulk. However, with their enemy so far above them, the real danger was the large target presented by their horses. The riders held to zigzagging patterns, but the Indian ponies were more adept at this than Riley's mount and the packhorse.

Blood thumped in Touch the Sky's temples as he clung to his palomino and felt her muscles working like well-oiled cables. A bullet creased his back like a white-hot wire of pain; another thumped into his rawhide shield. When the miners could see them coming, with Touch the Sky and Tom Riley out front, Caleb's men sent an offensive volley toward the ridge to take some pressure off the approaching riders.

Hastily, miners exposed themselves to fire in order to pull the pointed stakes clear of the approach. All four riders burst into the barricaded camp, wide-eyed but alive, and the defenders loosed a mighty roar.

"Well, it ain't two platoons of cavalry, but I'm damn glad to see you!" Caleb called out.

Suddenly, a fresh volley from above forced everyone to desperate cover. The new arrivals barely got their horses into the makeshift corral protected by a limestone outcropping and behind boulders or into rifle pits.

"How many you make up there?" Tom called out to his brother.

"Best guess is around fifty of 'em."

Fifty battle-hardened Southwest renegades, Touch the Sky thought. Each capable of getting off perhaps three shots a minute with a percussion rifle. But even more formidable was the fact that each wore a quiver stuffed with at least twenty-five arrows, and no doubt hundreds of spare arrows were held in reserve stacks.

"How many casualties down here?" Tom added.

"Three miners killed, six wounded, so far. And they killed Tilly Blackford."

"Little Sarah's ma? Jesus! How are the rest of the women and kids?"

Caleb and Touch the Sky both knew Tom was really asking how Kristen was doing. Caleb had to wait for the gunfire to slacken before he could answer.

"They're scared spitless—that's how they're doing. Snipers keep them confined to the houses. We've got some of that new canned milk of Gail

Borden's, but once it runs out the little ones are without milk. None of the beef cows can be butchered under fire, nor can we haul in any vegetables."

"Man alive," Tom said. "Talk about being trapped between a rock and a hard place!"

"Any shooting we do from down here is wasted," Caleb added. "If those renegades try to come down, raiding all at once or whatever, we can lay down some heavy fire. But we can't see enough from here to justify wasting the lead while they're up there. Besides, it's a bad angle. You have to break cover to get a bead on anything up there."

"Could a raiding party sneak up there?" Tom asked. "In the dark, I mean."

Touch the Sky answered this query himself. "It might get up there, but it would never get back down. These miners are no cowards; they'll do whatever you tell them. But not one of them is trained in night movement or combat. Those Kiowas and Comanches, on the other hand, are the best night fighters on the plains. They can steal a woman from her bed without waking up her husband."

"Besides," Caleb put in, "that's Sis-ki-dee and Big Tree up there. When it comes to dealing misery after sundown, those two are fish in water."

How well Touch the Sky could verify this fact! He remembered the long, brutal, agonizing night he had spent fighting both of them aboard the derailed orphan train full of terrorized children.

Again Two Twists complained about all their chattering in English. Touch the Sky translated the main points for his comrades. It was the

53

canny Little Horse who first suggested the germ of Touch the Sky's plan.

"Brother," he said, "it is true that we are trapped down here without supplies. But they are trapped up there too."

"Have you become the shaman?" Touch the Sky rebuked him. "Give over with this speaking in riddles."

"Think on it, buck," Little Horse said. "We have both crossed that ridge, have we not?"

"You know we have."

"*Ipewa*. Good. You know that rimrock up there; so you must also know there is no place to establish a base camp on it."

"No," Touch the Sky agreed. "The ridge is really only a narrow stone ledge with heaps of scree all behind it."

"As you say. Which has to mean, does it not, that they are unable to establish a base camp?"

"No," Touch the Sky said slowly, catching on to Little Horse's meaning. "They cannot. I see which way your thoughts roam."

"Damn," Tom complained, reminding Touch the Sky that he was truly at home in neither world, red man's or white man's, "I wish to hell you'd talk in English, Matthew."

"Little Horse was just pointing out that they don't have any room at all up there for a base camp."

"So what?" Caleb demanded. "We supposed to feel sorry for them?"

"That's not the point, yellow beard. This is a siege. A siege means they plan to dig in. That means a steady base of resupply. Without a base camp, and with Wendigo Mountain so close by, it's only logical that they'll get their provisions and ammunition by runners from the nearby camp."

"Yeah, so what? You mean we should gun for the runners?"

"No," Touch the Sky said. "Runners can be easily replaced. But a base camp is another matter."

"You mean—"

"I mean that a strong defense here in your camp won't get it done. Time is on their side, and time will whip you. Yes, you have to mount a strong defense, but there has to be an offensive strike too. We have to get on top of Wendigo Mountain and destroy their camp. Do that, and we destroy the siege."

Silence greeted this conclusion as Caleb and Tom considered it. Finally, Caleb said, "That shines right by me. But, Touch the Sky, you yourself tried to ride up that mountain and never made it. They'll have sentries on that slope, and even a few men could hold off an army from up there."

"Straight arrow," Touch the Sky said. "But they will not be watching the cliffs behind. That is how we will get up there."

Chapter Six

"I knew that White Man Runs Him would come flying this way," Wolf Who Hunts Smiling said, his words tipped with scorn. "His hair-face masters are up against it; so of course he must come to lick their spittle! But how did you let word get to the soldiertown? This blue blouse named Riley is a soldier to reckon with. They will be twice the trouble."

Wolf Who Hunts Smiling had ridden out from camp soon after Touch the Sky and his companions, eager to see how things were going up here in the Sans Arcs.

"You would tell us about this soldier?" Big Tree shot back. "Cheyenne, it was he and his men who dressed like hostages down in the Blanco Canyon country. We traded our Cheyenne prisoners for them only to end up in a hail of bullets."

Sis-ki-dee laughed at both of them. "Listen to

the scared girls huddling in their sewing lodge to shiver and quake! Big plans they had, and now one soldier leaps into the picture and they are ready to ride to the rear with the cowards!"

Big Tree, peering over the ridge to see how things stood below in the dark camp, turned to glower at the Contrary Warrior.

"Words are cheap coins, buck, spent freely by toothless old women. You took a Crow woman hostage when you fled from Touch the Sky into Bloody Bones Canyon. She was the only reason he spared your life. But you made one mistake, swollen boaster. In letting her go, you also spared a witness who has spread the tale of your blubbering cowardice across the Red Nation! 'Please, Touch the Sky!' you begged him. 'Please do not kill me!'"

Sis-ki-dee's scar-ravaged face went livid with rage while Wolf Who Hunts Smiling and Big Tree grinned at this rare show of vulnerability. But they both knew better than to push Sis-ki-dee too far.

"Will we scrap like dogs over meat?" Wolf Who Hunts Smiling demanded. "Now we know how the wind sets. Let us cease snarling at each other and turn our fight to our common enemy." A rifle cracked nearby as one of the renegades took aim below. "The high ground will not be enough. I know Touch the Sky, and I know this Tom Riley. And Caleb Riley too has grit to him. They will come at us. They will not sit down there and build their death wickiups. They mean to fight!"

"These are words I can pick up," Big Tree said. "They will fight. And when they do, it will be the unexpected. Soon it will be dark. I will give orders to double the guard below. They will give us

57

some merry sport, bucks. But this place hears me. We will all string our next bows with Touch the Sky's gut!"

No one knew better than the three Cheyenne braves what it would take to scale those cliffs behind Wendigo Mountain. They had done it once before, and it cost them not only the life of their companion Shoots the Bear—it proved to be the hardest struggle they had yet faced.

So Touch the Sky did not even consider making this an order. Indian leaders did not give orders as whiteskin leaders did; instead, they inspired their men by their own example. When a decision was to be reached, they tried to express the will of the group, not their own desires.

As darkness spread over the mining camp like a dark cloak, the three braves parleyed behind a spine of rocks.

"There are easier ways to die," Little Horse said. His bravado had been shaken from him by Touch the Sky's audacious suggestion. "But if we succeed, it will be important not only to the miners here."

Two Twists nodded. "As you say. The majority of their warriors are up on that ridge. The majority of their horses and equipment are not. We can destroy their ability to wage war for many moons to come. And that takes our camp out from under the shadow of attack, at least for a time."

"I am not eager to return to that death trap," Touch the Sky said. "It took our ancestors and it took our companion. It wants the rest of us too. But I see no use in huddling down here like rabbits cowering in a hole."

His companions nodded, but they also looked solemn at his reference to their ancestors. The Cheyennes, the Lakotas, the Arapahoes, even the mountain-loving Utes—all avoided Wendigo Mountain. It was said that any brave who touched the slope of that place would never leave it alive.

Everyone in the tribe knew the bloody and tragic history of Wendigo Mountain and the reason why it was taboo. A group of Cheyenne hunters, surrounded by murderous Crow Crazy Dogs, had fled into the Sans Arcs. Because it was the most formidable peak, they chose Wendigo Mountain. But due to the mists that always enshrouded it, they did not realize that the opposite side was sheer cliffs.

The relentless Crazy Dogs, highly feared suicide warriors, locked onto the Cheyenne like hounds on a blood scent. They backed them to the cliffs. The Cheyennes used all their musket balls and arrows. Then, rather than giving the Crazy Dogs the pleasure of torturing them, the Cheyennes all sang their death songs. As one, all twelve hunters locked arms and stepped off the cliffs. They were impaled on the basalt turrets far below; their bodies were never recovered.

Because the warriors died after dark and violently, they suffered especially bad deaths. Now all twelve were souls in torment, doomed to haunt Wendigo Mountain. It was said one could hear their groans in the moaning of the wind.

But like Touch the Sky, Little Horse and Two Twists saw the need to risk bad death yet again. They gave this plan grim nods, and Touch the Sky moved, leaping from boulder to boulder, then to the pile of timbers where Tom and Caleb huddled.

Tom was explaining the operation of the Parrot muzzle loader when the Cheyenne brave arrived. Touch the Sky quickly explained his plan.

"It's straight grain," Caleb said when the tall warrior fell silent. "An army travels on its stomach, and that includes an Injun army. Cut them off from pemmican and corn liquor, not to mention bullets and arrows, and they'll lose the sap for fighting."

"It's logical," Tom said. "But not if it's too dangerous to succeed. Can those cliffs be scaled, Touch the Sky?"

"We did it before. It'll be rough. But it's the last thing they'll be watching for. They'll be on that front slope."

Reluctantly, Tom nodded. "I think the risk is too great, but everything I've learned in the field tells me a multiple defense is the best. It's always good to strike at the unprotected flanks. Down here, hell, all we can do is react to what they choose to do. Your plan has the virtue of taking charge of the situation."

As if to verify his thoughts, a bullet struck close and made all three men duck.

"Listen," Tom said. "As long as you'll be sneaking out of camp anyway, any chance you'll put some of these in place?"

Tom nodded toward several nitroglycerin blocks, which were well-protected from bullets behind a pile of rocks. "We can prepare the charges now before it gets dark. I've got a whole spool of black-powder fuse. These should be planted about a couple hundred feet out, spanning the ground those renegades would have to cover if they decided to mass against us from below."

Touch the Sky nodded. Tom carefully removed the blocks from their cardboard containers and slid blasting caps into the cap wells on top of each. He crimped an end of fuse to each cap.

Touch the Sky and his companions prepared for their night mission as they had for so many others. First, Touch the Sky blackened their faces with charcoal. This move was more than practical; to a Cheyenne, the color black symbolized joy at the death of an enemy. Ideally, warriors would paint and fast before such a task, but this would have to do.

Next, each covered his head with a robe or blanket, leaving them wrapped for a long time as Uncle Moon climbed higher in the sky. The time spent doing this was amply rewarded, however, when they unwrapped their eyes. Vastly dilated pupils now squeezed the last particles of light from the air, and they could see shapes and outlines they had missed earlier.

Touch the Sky's companions had an acquaintance with various hair-face explosives. He quickly explained the blocks, and as each man took one, nervous sweat glistened on their faces.

Weapons would be a hindrance for the long climb up those cliffs; so their rifles were left behind. But they took their knives and bows, for they would be necessary to kill the guards up above. Caleb provided plenty of strong new rope, which the Cheyennes coiled securely around their bodies.

It was dark save for the foxfire glow of a quarter moon and the light of a starry dome far above the sawtooth mountain peaks. Up above, the renegades fired regularly to keep the whiteskins nervous. Now and then, a fire arrow flew in and set something ablaze. Then gutsy volunteers ran to douse the flames.

Touch the Sky and his companions fanned out on a line, a double arm's length between them, and slowly moved toward the only entrance into the camp. When they drew even with the last guard post established by the miners and faced the long talus slope to the base of the mountain, Touch the Sky again called his men around him.

"Plant your thunder blocks," he whispered. "Place stones over them. Make sure this"—he pointed to the blasting cap on his, which Tom had secured with twine—"is still in place and the fuse attached. Wait for me to make the owl hoot; then head down the slope. They are out there waiting for us; so keep your blade to hand."

His companions nodded. They were fully aware, as was he, that it was very bad medicine, the worst, to chance any risk after sundown. For the Cheyennes, as for most tribes, night belonged to the Wendigo, to the souls in torment, to *odjib*, the things made of smoke that could not be fought, but would fright a man to death.

Yet Touch the Sky carried the white man's ways in him, and he remembered the sayings John Hanchon taught him. One, especially, occurred to him now: *Needs must when the devil drives*. The whites too sometimes had truth firmly by the tail.

The devil right now was red, and his headquarters was on top Wendigo Mountain. They could stay here and hack at the branches of evil, or they could climb those cliffs and chop into its root.

They fanned out again and hid their charges in the dirt and stones. Touch the Sky then studied the slope in the darkness, his night-prepared vision assisting. He could spot no human shapes, but he knew, against this enemy, that meant nothing.

Fear throbbed in his palms, but he refused to let it master him. Instead, as old Arrow Keeper had taught him, he turned his fear into a thing he could place outside of himself.

He searched, listened, and even sniffed the air. Satisfied, he gave the owl hoot softly, and they moved out.

Every foot of that long, talus-strewn slope was gained in an agony of suspense, waiting for cold steel to cut or a Comanche skull cracker to dash the life out of them.

Crawling low to avoid a profile, moving when the wind picked up and covered his noise, Touch the Sky descended the mountain through the very heart of his enemy's best guards. Twice, he passed so close to renegades that he could smell the bear grease in their hair.

But he avoided any clashes since he knew full well the plan was doomed if Big Tree and Sis-ki-dee learned too soon that the Cheyennes had deserted the mining camp. A shout, or a dead body, would cause the same—failure.

He had not reckoned, however, on the many snakes who were nocturnal hunters. As he lay still at one point, waiting for some wind noise to cover his movement past a renegade guard, a scaly body suddenly tracked across his back!

Startled, he almost flinched, but caught himself. When he felt the weight on his back he realized that a snake had crawled onto him and was pausing to take warmth from him. But what kind of snake? Most up here were not poison, but some were, including the many rattlers drawn to these heights by mice and chipmunks.

Touch the Sky lay trapped, unable to move even when the wind conveniently gusted. If that snake was poison and bit him, he might survive; but he would surely be useless to complete this mission. However, his companions must be well out ahead of him by now. He could waste no more time.

Frustrated, he tried tensing and releasing, tensing and releasing his back muscles. The snake shifted, irritated, and Touch the Sky steeled himself for the long fangs.

However, the snake settled in again. Touch the Sky frowned, recalling all he could about snakes. He pictured this one in the darkness, head lifting, forked tongue sampling the air, gathering in odor particles . . . *odor particles!* He reminded himself that snakes had an especially keen sense of smell, and sudden new odors in their territory were interpreted as danger.

Every Cheyenne carried a few grayish-green leaves of the aromatic plant sage in his medicine pouch, for it was a versatile cooking herb. Moving slowly, cautiously, fearful of those fangs at any moment, Touch the Sky inched his right hand toward the rawhide pouch over his right hip.

He slid a dried leaf out, waited for the wind to pick up, then crumpled it between his fingers. Even he could smell the pungent odor, and the snake surely picked it up. Almost instantly its weight left his back.

He gave brief thanks to Maiyun, the Day Maker and protector of the red men. Then, moving out on his elbows and knees, heedless of the raw, throbbing cuts from rocks and stones, Touch the Sky moved forward to join his companions.

Chapter Seven

Dawn broke over the Sans Arcs range in its full glory, turning the sky over the peaks salmon pink. Kristen Steele, her eyes puffy from the growing dearth of rest and sleep, watched the dawn through a narrow space between her front door and the frame. For the moment, all was peaceful and still, and one might have believed life around here was normal again. Pockets of mist floated between the peaks like gossamer clouds of cotton. The dawn chorus of thousands of songbirds filled the camp with a warbling beauty. The air was still crisp and cool, but so pure it caressed the lungs.

But if this were a normal morning, Kristen reminded herself, the first whistle of the day would blow the signal for work to begin. The workday around here lasted from can to can't, as Caleb liked to say. Men would be streaming down the camp streets, carrying their helmets and joking to each other. And if this were a normal day, Woman Dress wouldn't be tending to two wounded men in her living room. Kristen's house had become a field hospital of sorts, and the wounded lay on cots or pallets of blankets and quilts.

"Tom and Caleb be here soon," Woman Dress said in her halting English. "Make coffee maybe better do?"

"Of course," Kristen said, hurrying to the Franklin stove in the little kitchen lean-to and building a fire under the pot.

As the water heated, she crossed to the back door, lifted the bar, and opening the door just a few inches to peer out. Two gray squirrels were playing on the big stump near the door. Kristen gazed at the long gully winding up through the trees to the ridge above. Maybe, she thought, she'd better mention that to Caleb and Tom. Maybe it—

Loud thumps on the front door interrupted her musings. She hurried back inside to let Caleb and Tom in. Both men looked exhausted. Beard stubble darkened Tom's sunburned face. They had been up all night, keeping an eye on the defenses. They had also found a sheltered spot to set up the Parrot artillery rifle on its big tripod mount. As the men waited, Kristen made sourdough biscuits and fried the last of her bacon.

"Sorry there isn't more meat," she apologized as she served the men. "And the flour will run out tomorrow."

"A lot of things will be running out pretty soon." Caleb closed his weary eyes for a long moment and massaged them with his thumbs. Then he opened his eyes and looked at his brother. "Let's just hope Touch the Sky and his men can pull this off. I'm thinking now that maybe we should have stopped them. It's damned risky."

"What?" Kristen demanded. "Pull what off? Where is Matthew?"

Tom glanced at her sharply for a moment, unable to hide his jealousy. Although he and Kristen had talked all around the subject of marriage, an understanding of sorts had grown up between them. He knew she had once loved the Cheyenne; indeed, their forbidden love was the reason Matthew Hanchon had given up the white man's world for the red. But Touch the Sky was married now, a father; yet Kristen's worried tone made it clear she still harbored strong feelings for the brave.

As Caleb explained the plan to route the renegades, Kristen and Woman Dress both turned pale at the thought of the danger those three Cheyenne faced. But before Kristen could say anything, Dakota Boggs's voice sang out from outside the front door.

"Caleb! Harney Robinson just caught a round in his belly! It's bad. We can't move him. We got him inside my place, but he needs doctorin' damn quick!"

"I'll go." Kristen immediately gathered up her bandages and a little pail of solution of gentian.

"Not by yourself." Tom pushed away from his plate. He clapped on his hat and checked the loads in his Colt Cavalry Model. Then he and Kristen joined Dakota in the fortified camp street.

Everywhere, men were huddling behind barricades and glancing up toward the ridges surrounding them. Here and there, partially burned buildings showed blackened corners or roofs. Dakota's little bungalow hunkered about six houses down the line. As they moved quickly across the open space, Tom glanced overhead constantly. They were about halfway to their destination when the renegades decided to unleash another furious volley.

So many rifles detonated that the barrage sounded like an ice floe breaking apart. Sudden, intense screaming erupted from women and children. Kristen was not one to swoon in an emergency, but the suddenness of the attack made her scream and cling to Tom. As bullets kicked up plumes all around their feet, Dakota leapt for the corner of the nearest house, and Tom pushed Kristen to safety under an abandoned freight wagon.

"Christ!" Tom said. "They're focusing their fire on one of the houses!"

Kristen saw what he meant. After the initial sweep of the camp, the renegades had settled their aim on one house about thirty feet ahead of them.

"That's Dot Perkins and her kids trapped in there!" she cried out. "Terry and Jenny are in my class! Oh, Tom, look! They're sending fire arrows down again too!"

Riley had seen and heard enough. Cursing out loud, he suddenly broke from cover and started running headlong down the street.

"Tom!" Kristen cried out. "Tom! What are you doing?"

Behind her, the door to her house slapped open and Caleb leapt out into the street. He raced after his brother. Kristen watched both of them cut toward the long limestone outcropping that ran like a shelf over the north side of the camp. Then she realized that the artillery rifle was set up there!

Kristen watched Tom sight in while Caleb dropped one of the long shells down the muzzle. There was a roar, followed by a long white trail of smoke; then a resounding explosion knocked a chunk of the ridge loose. Kristen had the satisfaction of seeing several Indians tumble down with the debris. Tom had scored a direct hit on one of the most dangerous nests of snipers.

After that brief moment of triumph, a cheer boiled through the camp, and the Indian volley fell silent. But moments later, another spate of burning arrows poured in from other positions, and the men fell silent as they rushed to douse the new fires.

Once they had negotiated their exit from the mining camp, Touch the Sky and his companions faced a hard journey on foot. Never could they have gotten their ponies out of camp, nor was there any place to tether them at the base of Wendigo Mountain.

Fortunately, both Touch the Sky and Little Horse knew this country well from sighting the spur-line railroad through. Relying on good maps provided by their memory, they were able to avoid many of the pitfalls of this rugged terrain: the huge piles of scree and glacial morraine; the steep ridges that wore a man down and led nowhere; the spring-swollen streams that soaked a man's powder and left him shivering in raw night winds. While the moon clawed higher toward its zenith, they crossed the front slope of

Wendigo Mountain and slogged through scree and basalt turrets. Finally, they reached the sheer cliffs behind even as Sister Sun rose from her bed in the eastern sky.

Chafing at the delay, Touch the Sky nonetheless knew they must wait until late in the day before beginning their ascent. Otherwise, they might break through the protective belt of mist above into sight of an alert sentry while it was still light enough to spot them.

They badly needed rest anyway. The trio pitched a cold camp in a well-protected hollow near the cliffs. But rest could never come easy to a Cheyenne in that unholy place. Not only were they surrounded by the bones of their comrades, but the terrible shrieking of those winds up on the cliffs rubbed their nerves raw. These were not winds at all, but eerie human cries, cries of pain and desolation—and of warning.

How many wise Indians, Touch the Sky could not help wondering, had heard that warning and heeded it? As for his band, not one brave here had ever shown the white feather. All had been tested and tested again in hard battles, even young Two Twists. Each was a warrior; none better could have been found in the Red Nation.

And yet, this climb ahead of them was a different type of foe. Touch the Sky's two companions had grown up believing that Wendigo Mountain was a place of terror, suffering, and death—a place to be avoided at all costs. "If you do not behave," Cheyenne mothers often threatened their children, "I'll send you to Wendigo Mountain." Not just a hard climb and a hard enemy waited above, powerful bad medicine loomed ahead as well.

The three Cheyennes prepared as best they could. Their animal-tendon bowstrings were tightened and inspected for frayed spots. They had no idea what might be encountered above or how long they might be pinned down. So they had stuffed their parfleches and legging sashes with dried venison and strips of cloth Caleb gave them for binding wounds. Remembering how hard the last climb was on their feet, they stuffed their moccasins with dried grass to soften the sharp edges.

Now and then, as they waited for the sun to sink lower in the west, a vagrant wind gust brought them the faint sound of battle from the distant mining camp. When their shadows began to slant toward the east, Touch the Sky gave the nod. Their final preparations could begin.

According to their custom, each brave said a brief, silent battle prayer as he touched his personal medicine and the totem of his clan. Touch the Sky had no official clan, but Arrow Keeper had presented him with a set of badger claws—the totem of Chief Running Antelope of the Northern Cheyenne. He had been killed in the year the white man's winter count called 1840, the year Touch the Sky had been born. Arrow Keeper had called this chief Touch the Sky's father, and the warrior had never known Arrow Keeper to speak bent words.

"Brother," Little Horse said curiously, watching his friend remove the badger claws and pray over them. "I would ask you a thing."

"I have ears."

"Brother, we have saved each other's life too many times to count up. We have fought bluecoats and whiskey traders and land-grabbers and

Pawnees. We have fought all of them side by side and then smeared our bodies with their blood. We have stood shoulder to shoulder at the Buffalo Battle and sent many white hiders' souls across the Great Divide. So tell me only this.

"You know that I have seen the mark of the warrior buried in your hair. That arrow point is so perfect it might have been fashioned by Maiyun, the Day Maker. And I recall when the Bull Whips set upon you during the buffalo hunt and beat you after Wolf Who Hunts Smiling played the fox and accused you of violating Hunt Law. You told them your father was a great warrior, greater than any in our tribe."

Touch the Sky nodded. "Certainly I too recall this. The Bull Whips mocked me for a liar."

"They did. But others did not. You fight like five men. Clearly, you descend from a stout warrior's loins! But, brother, when you sought your great vision at Medicine Lake, was it revealed to you the part you are meant to play in our tribe's destiny? How much was made known to you?"

Touch the Sky thought about these questions for some time. While he did, he sharpened his obsidian knife and listened to the distant gunfire.

"Much was revealed," he finally answered. "But it was like shadow pictures on snow. The shape of things was there, but not the substance."

If this answer confused Little Horse, he did not show it. He merely nodded, accepting these words. "Truly, I have heard that visions and medicine dreams convey great truths, yet little that can be told with words."

"As you say. They are felt more than known. But now, buck, let us both give over with words." Touch the Sky nodded toward the cliffs. "It is

73

time. Wendigo Mountain is waiting for us. We have a hard climb ahead, and no doubt a hard fight waits for us at the top. So from here on out, let our thoughts be bloody and nothing else."

Chapter Eight

Taking a grim revenge for the braves killed by that big-thundering artillery gun, the renegades hammered at the mining camp throughout the day. Big Tree and Sis-ki-dee had learned from the white Comancheros in their desert homeland how to make gun cotton. They simply dipped tow cloth into a mixture of niter, sulfur, and naphtha supplied by the slave-trading Comancheros in exchange for Indian captives. Wrapped around their arrows, the gun cotton could be hurled into the camp below, where it would spew flames everywhere.

All day long, the renegades menaced the camp and forced men from shelter to fight the flames. Then they would open fire on the beleagured hair faces. Several more of the whites had been killed or wounded. Yet return fire directed up toward the ridge was mostly wasted—with the exception of that artillery rifle. That weapon had the capacity to blow the very ridge out from under the Indians' feet. So the renegades showed more caution and spread out even farther apart.

As the sun began to cast fiery embers on the western horizon, Big Tree said, "The big-talking gun has been silent for some time now. Perhaps they are out of shells for it."

"No." Sis-ki-dee shook his raggedly cropped head. "Tom Riley hauled that gun in. He would not have carried it this far just to fire it a few times. He is conserving his shots. By fighting the Sioux he has learned their maxim: One bullet, one enemy."

While Sis-ki-dee spoke, he was straining to see how things looked over among the cluster of houses on one side of camp. One house was still on fire and others smoked from continual assaults of gun cotton.

Big Tree laughed. "Look at the Red Peril! His loins ache for his sun-haired white woman. He is worried that perhaps she was killed before he could top her and sate his lust!"

"And you would not top her, I suppose?"

Big Tree shrugged. "She is just one more woman. All cats look alike in the dark. I value a lame horse over a comely woman."

"She is not just one more woman. The tall one once held her in his blanket for love talk. He has risked his life for her before, and she is one reason why he is here now."

"Never mind the woman," Big Tree said. He too had been scouring the area below, but not to look for women. "Answer this. Why have we not seen one sign of those three Cheyennes all this day long?"

This question made Sis-ki-dee's scar-ravaged face compress itself into a frown. "Why indeed?" he said, watching his companion warily. "And now let me meet question with question. Why has not one arrow flown up here to answer ours?"

Both braves stared below, their cocky smiles replaced by speculative frowns. Finally, Sis-ki-dee said, "We have not seen them because they have sneaked out of the camp."

"But why?"

"It is pointless to come up here," Big Tree said. "They are three against a legion."

"Then where?" Sis-ki-dee asked. Even as he finished asking, both renegades turned their heads to the left toward Wendigo Mountain. A queasiness invaded their stomachs as they guessed the truth.

"They mean to cut off our tail while our teeth are gnashing," Big Tree said. "They have gone to destroy our camp!"

Sis-ki-dee tried to shrug that explanation off. "So? Let them try! They will never get up that slope alive. We left enough sentries there."

"We did," Big Tree said. "On the slope. But what if they have dared the cliffs behind?"

Sis-ki-dee could say nothing to this query. Against all odds, those plucky Cheyennes had climbed the cliffs once before. That they might do so again had not occurred to him until now, and all of a sudden, he realized the danger he and his band faced.

"You have truth firmly by the tail, buck," Sis-ki-dee said. "I will pick a few men and—"

"You will not," Big Tree said. "You had your chance at Bloody Bones Canyon, and you squandered it. It is my turn to make Touch the Sky's life a hurting place. And I will take no men. I will ride alone."

When Sis-ki-dee started to object, Big Tree said, "What about your play pretty down below, stag-in-rut? How will you mount her from Wendigo Mountain? Leave me here, and I assure you, she will be cold as a wagon wheel by the time you return. I will surely kill her along with the rest."

"Then go," Sis-ki-dee said. "But whatever you do, do not let that Cheyenne dog gain our camp. If he destroys our horses and powder cache, we will be grizzly bears without teeth or claws."

Big Tree caught up his buckskin mustang and started across the face of the mountains. Since he stuck to well-known trails his men had blazed throughout this area, he was able to make far better time than he could on foot. By the time darkness had claimed the sky, he had rounded Wendigo Mountain and reached the base of the cliffs.

Slowly, while the wind howled and shrieked around him, he threaded his way through the many basalt turrets, searching for sign. However, if his enemies had been this way, they had covered their trail completely.

Big Tree reined in at the very base of the cliffs and gazed thoughtfully overhead. Had he perhaps guessed wrong? It would have been an agonizing climb. Should he bother to take the time to circle back around and ascend that long slope, just to warn them up above? If his enemies were climbing these cliffs, he could easily beat them. Perhaps he should—

Abruptly, a pebble landed at Big Tree's moccasined feet. A few heartbeats later, another pebble fell. His huge, weather-beaten face creased in a grin of triumph. The Cheyenne dogs were up there, all right. And since they would not have started until late, they could not be that far up yet. Now there would be some merry sport!

Big Tree grabbed a handful of his pony's roached mane, meaning to swing up and ride like the wind around to the front. His companions must be warned. But something occurred to him. Why not begin the sport right now? Besides, it was better if the three Cheyennes realized they had been discovered. They might abandon their plan and come down. Still grinning, Big Tree reached one hand over his shoulder and grabbed a bunch of new pine-shaft arrows from his quiver.

The winds that buffeted Wendigo Mountain always howled like souls in pain. But added to this misery were intermittent, lashing rains—cold rains that soaked the three warriors and chilled them to violent shivers after the sun went down.

The Powder River Cheyennes were up against it in the truest sense. The arduous climb was dangerous and exhausting. So much so that, at the beginning, Touch the Sky had almost called off his crazy plan. But the young warrior had learned one thing well. Trouble never went away on its own if he ran from it. He either had to take it by the horns or suffer a hard goring. If the warriors could not get up there and destroy the renegades' base of operations, the Northern Plains would belong to Wolf Who Hunts Smiling and his murdering cohort.

Progress was agonizingly slow. Every finger length was eked out at the cost of unbelievable sweat and toil. Touch the Sky had the longest arms; so he went up first, clawing for handholds, groping constantly for toeholds on the smooth limestone expanse. Each time he reached a spur or occasional stunted tree or bush, he carefully tested its strength. Then he secured a rope to it. Little Horse followed, then Two Twists.

Despite the cold, salty and stinging sweat beaded up on Touch the Sky's scalp and then rolled into his eyes. The fierce winds fanned the sweat, causing him to shake violently.

A few inches, another foot, and now the cliff face was so smooth it seemed as if farther advance was impossible. But Touch the Sky willed himself higher and refused to give up. Fingers and toes seeming to make their own holds, he somehow inched his way up that smooth stretch.

Little Horse and Two Twists were having a rough time. Shorter of limb, they found it even harder than he did to stretch between the scant holds. Touch the Sky knew he had to get a rope tied to something or his plan was smoke behind them. They could not continue to climb on air! Lightning flashed between rain squalls, and the brave could see his companions' faces below, ashen with fear and effort.

"Brothers!" he shouted down to them, his voice sounding tiny in the immensity of the constant wind. "We are the fighting Cheyennes! Hang on a bit longer, and we will reach easier going. I will throw the ropes down to you then!"

Muscles straining like guy ropes, Touch the Sky scrambled for some kind of hold. Above, perhaps ten handbreadths away, he spotted a small rock spur. If only he could reach it in time. But his assurance to his companions was proving easier to shout than to carry out.

"Brother!" Little Horse said in a desperate voice.

Touch the Sky looked down; then he felt his blood seem to stop and flow backward in his veins. Two Twists had slipped, and now he held on by only one foot and one hand. He pressed close to the rock face, but the rapacious wind threatened at every moment to tear him loose and hurtle him to the basalt turrets below.

"Hold on!" Touch the Sky shouted. "I will have a rope down in a little!"

Desperation welled up inside the brave. How many times had young Two Twists faced the Grim Warrior Death to prove his loyalty? How many times had his battlefield bravery, his habit of mocking the enemy to their face, inspired his comrades to the extra effort that decided the victory? And now he was about to plunge to his death right in front of the man he had always served without question.

Touch the Sky grasped, clawed, grasped again, and somehow found holds where none existed. His fingernails had torn loose long ago. Spidery lines of blood spread from his fingertips all the way down his arms. But the rock spur was just above him. And now his bones turned to stone when he heard Two Twists chanting the death song! Touch the Sky, face frozen with desperate urgency, unlooped his rope. Then he flung it up toward the spur—and missed!

He didn't realize it when he cussed in English. He tossed the rope up again and this time snared the spur. Working with desperate haste, willing

Judd Cole

his fingers to a machinelike efficiency, he knotted the rope.

"Watch out, Little Horse!" he shouted.

Touch the Sky tossed the rope past his companion. It reached Two Twists just as the young warrior lost his battle with gravity. Even as he began plummeting to his death, the rope slapped him in the face. Two Twists instinctively grabbed at it, missed, then grabbed once more. A second later, the rope snapped taut and held, and Two Twists dangled safely though somewhat shaken from the impact when he swung back into the face of the cliff.

For some time, all three braves held motionless, recovering from the near miss and steeling their nerves for more climbing. It was a slow and agonizing process getting Little Horse and Two Twists up to this stretch where, Touch the Sky knew from experience, the going got a bit easier. Little Horse climbed to the level of the rock spur; then Two Twists followed.

"I was in no trouble," Two Twists boasted, showing bravado to cover his understandable fear. "My only concern is that All Behind Him here"—he swatted Little Horse on his ample rump—"might fall on me."

"Once again," Little Horse said, "the calf bellows to the bull!"

Despite his exhaustion and apprehension—or maybe because of them—Touch the Sky flashed a rueful grin. "Never mind the chatter, you two jays. If you survive this, you can kill each other at your leisure."

He fell silent, squinting at a spot just below them. It was foolish, of course. But Touch the

82

Sky could almost swear he had seen sparks fly from the face of the—

There! There it was again. Sparks.

Something tickled his left ear. More sparks flew into his eyes. And then, with a sinking feeling in his belly like a chunk of cold lead, he realized that arrows were pelting them! And the sparks were because these arrows were special Comanche arrows tipped with white man's sheet iron, not flint. Iron tips bent and clinched when they hit bone, making them much more deadly.

Touch the Sky had no time to wonder how the renegades had guessed their plan. A Comanche could launch a big handful of arrows in mere seconds, and the sheer number coming in now, obviously launched from the base of the cliff, turned the air deadly all around them.

Finally, the barrage slowed and seemed to stop. Touch the Sky, holding his next breath, finally began to expel it in relief. Suddenly, one final arrow found them. And Touch the Sky heard the sickening noise, like an ax cutting a side of meat, as the iron-tipped arrow sliced into Little Horse's calf.

Chapter Nine

"Plenty Coups," Sis-ki-dee called out to one of his men. "I am going down below to scout. I will descend behind the houses. They have sentries walking. Have some of the men keep up a sporadic fire until I return. I want them to worry about the opposite end of the camp; so this time direct fire arrows and bullets at that end."

Plenty Coups nodded, though the Blackfoot lackey knew full well his leader had no reason to scout. They had done all the scouting they needed long ago. Sis-ki-dee had fire in his loins, and he was scouting for the woman who would put out the fire.

"Do not hold one position," Sis-ki-dee said. "That will give them a bead with the thunder gun. Shoot and then each time move to a new position."

Plenty Coups and several other braves moved

forward in the darkness, taking up positions at the rim. They were safe now; no one could see to draw a bead on them in this blackness.

Sis-ki-dee left his North & Savage rifle in its sheath, opting only for his bone-handled knife. He moved northwest along the high ridge, nearing the spot where that gully snaked down among the houses. His mastery of movement and hiding had already gotten him close enough to find out where Kristen Steele lived. The Crow Indian woman was staying with her during this emergency.

That thought prompted a smile from Sis-ki-dee. They were both beauties. Perhaps he could enjoy one of them down below and take one with him for later. And when he and Big Tree tired of her, they would let the men line up for her.

As Sis-ki-dee had ordered, his men opened up on the dark, quiet camp below. He watched bright orange flames arc out over the rim and plummet into the wagons, buildings, and numerous stacks of timber dotting the business end of camp. When Sis-ki-dee was sure the roving sentries would be down there fighting flames, he began his descent down the steep erosion gully.

It was hard going, even for one as seasoned to adverse climbs as he. At some points, he was forced to rig a rope to a stunted bush or a fat rock and lower himself foot by foot. He gave up any idea of bringing a woman back up this way. He would enjoy them and then kill them. The scalp of the blond woman, especially, would fetch much praise and trade high.

Soon enough, Sis-ki-dee could glimpse lantern light leaking under the edge of the back door of a house. It was built on a slant with the bottom of the ridge. Now the going was easy, and he had merely to brace his leg muscles against gravity. In the grainy blackness, he moved from rock to rock until he was only a stone's throw from the house. He slid his knife from his sash and settled in for a long moment to watch before he made his final move.

Tom and Caleb Riley, holed up with some of the wounded in Kristen's house, had been grabbing a few minutes of fitful sleep when the latest attack opened up.

"Damn," Caleb said, groping for his rifle. "Don't those featherheads ever sleep? Liam's on watch. Should we leave it to him?"

"I trust Liam," Tom said, peeking out the front door and watching the new flames at the far end of the street. "But we'd better head out. This might be a softening attack before they rush the entrance."

This thought sobered Caleb. After all, his brother hadn't won a brevet promotion for clerking duties. The two brothers hurried down to the sheltered position of the artillery rifle. All around them, men directed by Liam McKinney and others fought the flames with buckets of water and shovelfuls of dirt.

"Liam!" Caleb shouted above the din of shouting men and crackling flames. "Throw up a skirmish line across the front of camp, and dig in good. They might be attacking in force this time!"

Caleb and Tom took up their position at the Parrot, ensconced under a limestone outcropping. Then Caleb said, "Can you get a bead?"

"They won't let me. I can tell from watching the dispersal pattern that they're staying in motion as they shoot. This little puppy has taught them some deep respect for white man's technology. Won't do us much good in the dark, though. Unless—"

"Unless what?" When Tom waited a while before he answered, Caleb said, "Dammit! You've always done that, Tom! Always makin' a man beg you to know what's on your damned mind!"

"Quit whining, little brother, and listen up. They're moving around, all right. But they're confining their movement to that one section of the ridge between the south end and the spot where it forms a notch just off to our right. See? Regular as Big Ben."

"Yeah. Well, so what?"

"You're a damn good miner, Caleb, and you got a hell of a hard-hitting right fist. But you're poor shakes as a soldier. Look at this thing in terms of known facts and possible results. We now know for a fact that a good number of them are concentrated in a finite area—an area we have measured exactly, right?"

Caleb was starting to twig the game, and his temples were pulsing at the prospects. "Right. Don't whack the cork on me now, Cap'n."

"We haven't got many shells. But this gal fires as quick as you can drop ammo down the muzzle. If I traverse this barrel on an exact line with that one section of the ridge while you drop beans down the tube quick, we can blow a good section of the landscape right out from under them. I think four shells will do it. That leaves us with only three rockets, but it's a calculated risk. We not only discourage them from night harassment; we may even take out a good chunk of their man power."

"But if it doesn't work," Caleb muttered, "we're sitting on damn few shells if they attack down here later."

"True. But our friends up topside don't know how many shells we have. By not firing, we drop a hint that we're low. By blasting away now, we create the impression that we've got lots more where that came from."

Caleb nodded. Both points made sense. But he sure would have felt easier knowing they had more shells on hand. The savages obviously respected that gun.

"Dammit," Caleb said. "I wonder how Touch the Sky is doing?"

"He'll do his job or die trying. But we can't count on him. We have to fend for ourselves. Every man has to pack his own gear, or it won't get done. Not against these Indians, Caleb. They wiped out half the white population in Texas before they rode up here."

Reluctantly, Caleb agreed. "All right, big brother," he said, grabbing a shell. "It's time to kiss the mistress!"

Tom wrapped the lanyard around his hand and waited for the shell to slide home solidly. Then he double-checked his elevation and windage settings; he had calculated them during daylight hours and knew the exact setting for this distance. Satisfied, he jerked the lanyard and the first rocket whooshed toward its target, trailing blue-green fire.

Again, again, and yet again rockets were launched, four in total, the explosions so close together they seemed to come as one. As they detonated above, the Riley boys had the pleasure of hearing the miners cheer and of seeing tall geysers of dirt, rock, and shocked Indians blown off the ridge.

Satisfied that no sentries roamed close by, Sis-ki-dee had emerged from hiding and covered the remaining distance to the small lodge. Though the windows were reinforced with boards, wide cracks had been left. He peered through one and studied the interior.

It was hardly more luxurious than some Indian lodges he had seen, though cleaner and neater. He glanced past a kitchen with a hand pump and crossed-stick shelves. In the bigger room, make-shift beds had been arranged on the floor, and several wounded hair faces occupied them. They were either asleep or unconscious. And there was the golden-haired beauty, bent over one of them to administer white man's medicine from a dark brown bottle.

How noble, he thought, a sneer dividing his face in the moonlit darkness. Like Touch the Sky, whom she probably still loved even though he had a red wife and babe. Filled with light and reason and hope and all the other claptrap taught by their white medicine men who preached about a loving God. There was only one God among the white men, and his name was Sam Colt. The gun was the only deity that mattered out here.

Woman Dress was nowhere in sight, but Sis-ki-dee didn't worry about her. Nor would those wounded men pose much trouble. He moved to the corner of the house, intending to go round to the front door. They would expect no Indians in camp now, and the sun-haired beauty would no doubt open the door at his knock—if it was even locked. He could pull her out into the street and take her there on the ground like a common animal to humiliate her even more.

He had just started his final move when the sky overhead and to his right suddenly exploded in blinding light. Startled, Sis-ki-dee looked up just in time to see some of his men thrown from the ridge. Those four quick explosions had been masterfully timed and placed; within moments, Sis-ki-dee heard the shrill piping of an eagle-bone whistle. One of his men was calling desperately to him. His men were not squaws, quick to panic. It must be bad indeed up there.

Sis-ki-dee cursed. If Plenty Coups had been killed, they were without a leader. And in the ensuing panic of those explosions, who knew what mistake they might make? His men feared little, but most of them had been stringing their bows with both hands when brains were passed out.

There was nothing else for it. He would have to forego his pleasure this time. But he swore by the four directions that he would merge his flesh with Kristen Steele's before he slid his knife under that scalp the color of new wheat.

"It has struck bone," Touch the Sky said grimly.

The rains had stopped some time ago, but the wind still howled and raged like berserk warriors. It clawed at them, trying to pry them loose from their precarious holds on the side of Wendigo Mountain.

Going mostly by touch, severely hampered in his cramped and tentative position, Touch the Sky had quickly examined Little Horse's wound. The stout brave had not lost his hold when struck; however, weakened by the fierce pain and growing blood loss, Little Horse must surely be forced to soon let go and plunge to his death.

Two Twists too managed to work in close to his companions. All three of them knew the importance of Touch the Sky's words about the point striking bone. That sheet iron would surely have clinched. Merely snapping off the arrow and pushing it through would be disastrous in this case.

"Never mind," Little Horse said, his voice spiked with pain. "I am dead, brothers, but you are not! Move on, both of you, and take the fight to the cricket-eating vermin above! I have lived well, and I will die well. When I fall from this cliff, I will not scream in terror. I will curse the name of my enemies with my last breath since I cannot fall on their bones."

"Listen to All Behind Him strut and pose," Two Twists said with brash desperation, trying to hide his fear that Little Horse might soon die. "Now that he has to hang on, he regrets all the rich gall bladders and livers and intestines he gorged on all winter."

But even as he spoke, Two Twists wasted no time. While Touch the Sky removed his knife and prepared for some desperate surgery, the younger brave was rigging a rope around Little Horse. It was not easy work on this precarious cliff. But somehow Two Twists got a rope around his friend and then tied it around himself.

"Throw me the other end, buck!" Touch the Sky yelled. He too secured himself to Little Horse. No words were needed. All three knew what they intended. Little Horse would surely pass out at the intense pain, and all of his weight

would become the burden of his companions—
or so they thought.

"Cut those ropes," Little Horse ordered Two
Twists. His friends were barely holding on themselves; he had no intention of dragging them to
their death with him.

"Cut a cat's tail," Two Twists defied him, even
as he tightened the knot.

"Touch the Sky," Little Horse said, "cut those
ropes, or I will not let you cut my leg! I will not
let my companions die."

"The white men have a saying," Touch the Sky
said as he maneuvered into position to make the
first cut. "Teach your grandmother to suck eggs.
I am cutting that arrow point out, and we are
leaving the ropes on. Now hold quiet or I will
push all three of us off to shut you up."

Touch the Sky flinched when, abruptly, another flurry of arrows rained in.

"Arrows fly two ways," Two Twists said an-
grily, slewing around to grab a few from his
pouch. In a moment, he sent them flying toward
the ground.

"Hurry, brother," Little Horse urged Touch the
Sky. "I am keen for some diversion!"

Touch the Sky had only been joking. But now,
as he moved his body into position, he feared he
really might send them all falling. The arrow
point had entered the solid part of Little Horse's
calf, ripping muscle fibers and then clamping
around the bone.

Touch the Sky had once watched a white doctor remove one of these arrows. The trick was to
unbend the clinched metal with the very tip of
the knife, much as one might pry back the little
nubbins holding on a can lid. But he would have

to cut deep and work with brutal swiftness. He had cloths to bind the wound, but already blood loss was considerable.

Each brave wore a leather band around his left wrist to protect it from the slap of his bowstring. Two Twists removed his now and inserted it between Little Horse's teeth.

Touch the Sky pushed his knife into the ragged wound, and Little Horse jerked violently. Showing no mercy, since conditions hardly permitted it, the desperate Cheyenne probed deeper. He was severely hampered by having only one hand available, the other clinging tenaciously to a crevice. This meant that he had to probe with the knife, then stop and use his fingers to feel his way since light was insufficient.

Touch the Sky worked as quickly as possible, praying all the while that Maiyun would bless his clumsy fingers. Little Horse was losing far too much blood now.

Touch the Sky and Two Twists kept expecting sudden weight to challenge them as Little Horse sagged. But though Little Horse grunted hard, flinched often, and came close to oblivion, he fought it off. He had meant what he said about refusing to risk his friends.

At last, Touch the Sky eased the mangled metal point out and quickly bound his friend's wound. Two Twists took the leather band from his mouth.

"When are you going to start?" Little Horse said weakly. "We can't dawdle here all night."

All three Cheyennes mocked death and shared a laugh at their comrade's joke. But before they began their laborious ascent again, Two Twists handed something to Touch the Sky. He glanced down in the dim moonlight, and pride and respect swelled his heart at this vivid proof of Little Horse's bottomless courage. The thick leather had been bitten clean through.

Chapter Ten

Big Tree did not count how many arrows he launched up the face of that cliff. It was his habit to always wear two quivers, both stuffed tight with carefully wrought arrows. His first flurry upward emptied perhaps half a quiver.

Big Tree remained well back from the cliff until the last of his spent arrows had clattered back to ground. He hurried forward to salvage those that had not broken because he spent far too much time fashioning each arrow to waste them lightly.

He was stuffing the last of them back into the foxskin quiver when he felt something wet drip onto his shoulder—something wet and still warm. He rubbed some onto his fingertips and smelled it in the darkness. An ear-to-ear smile suddenly divided his face when he recognized the familiar odor of blood. At least one of his arrows had scored!

If the hit had been fatal, his enemies had somehow caught the body. More likely it was a wound. But on that sheer cliff, even a mild wound took on dangerous new facets.

Perhaps he had even wounded Touch the Sky, the one Pawnees called, in hushed and respectful tones, the Bear Caller. They swore by the four directions that he had once summoned a grizzly bear to attack a Pawnee war party. But only look at the Pawnee tribe—once mighty warriors, they were now called the drunken fools of the plains, debauched as they were by devil water.

The mighty Bear Caller too, Big Tree gloated, was destined to be reduced. True, Big Tree mightily enjoyed mocking Sis-ki-dee's recent humiliation at Touch the Sky's hands. But the truth cried out in his inescapable memory. He had supped full of humiliations heaped on by Touch the Sky.

He had sat immobile, taken completely by surprise, when Touch the Sky killed his chief, Iron Eyes, and stole Honey Eater back from the Comancheros. And when Big Tree had launched an arrow into Touch the Sky's chest at point-blank range, the Cheyenne had flinched just enough to keep the point out of his heart. And that first climb the Cheyennes made up Wendigo Mountain—one of them had died, yes. But the other four had broached the renegade camp and got their Medicine Arrows back, killing a score of renegades in the process.

All these reasons, and several more, made Big Tree at least as keen as Sis-ki-dee to rip the Cheyenne's warm and beating heart out. And catalog-

A SPECIAL OFFER FOR LEISURE WESTERN READERS ONLY!

Get FOUR FREE Western Novels

Travel to the Old West in all its glory
and drama—without leaving your home!

GET YOUR 4 FREE BOOKS NOW—
A VALUE BETWEEN $16 AND $20
Mail the Free Book Certificate Today!

FREE BOOKS CERTIFICATE!

YES! I want to subscribe to the Leisure Western Book Club. Please send my 4 FREE BOOKS. Then, each month, I'll receive the four newest Leisure Western Selections to preview FREE for 10 days. If I decide to keep them, I will pay the Special Members Only discounted price of just $3.36 each, a total of $13.44. This saves me between $3 and $6 off the bookstore price. There are no shipping, handling or other charges. There is no minimum number of books I must buy and I may cancel the program at any time. In any case, the 4 FREE BOOKS are mine to keep—at a value of between $17 and $20! Offer valid only in the USA.

Name_____

Address_____

City_____ State_____

Zip_____ Phone_____

Biggest Savings Offer!

For those of you who would like to pay us in advance by check or credit card—we've got an even bigger savings in mind. Interested? Check here. ☐

If under 18, parent or guardian must sign.
Terms, prices and conditions subject to change. Subscription subject to acceptance. Leisure Books reserves the right to reject any order or cancel any subscription.

GET FOUR BOOKS TOTALLY *FREE*—A VALUE BETWEEN $16 AND $20

ing all his grievances also inspired Big Tree to empty the rest of one quiver. Big Tree waited for more blood. This time, however, a return flurry of hard-hitting arrows made him duck back, grinning at the sport.

If Big Tree's enemies wasted precious arrows like that, they must be angry. That meant the wound Big Tree had inflicted was serious. Good. He was here to make their world a hurting place, and this was only the beginning.

The three Cheyenne warriors knew they had been discovered, Big Tree reasoned as he caught up his buckskin and slid her hackamore on. But he knew the tall one was resolute of purpose, a trait learned from his white masters. Once Touch the Sky determined on a course of action, he generally completed it.

No, the warriors meant to gain the summit and wreak havoc on that camp. But Big Tree knew he could easily beat them to the top by riding unchallenged up the front slope.

For a moment, he felt as elated as he had when, still a boy, he watched his first torture of white captives in Texas. No tribe took such extreme pleasure at inflicting pain as did the Comanches. The torture of a white child was a festive event that sometimes lasted three days. And the idea of inflicting pain on these Northern Cheyennes held even more pleasure.

Big Tree rubbed his hand in the blood on his shoulder, then smeared it all over his face. Touch the Sky's or not, at least it was Cheyenne blood. Then he kicked his pony's flanks hard with both heels, racing to intercept his enemies.

* * *

"Over here," Sis-ki-dee told Plenty Coups. "In the light. I want to show you something."

Plenty Coups had barely escaped death when the whites blew that ridge out from under the Indians. But he had watched at least five companions tumble screaming to their deaths below. Now fear still held him in its grip as he obeyed his leader.

Sis-ki-dee had a small firepit burning well back from the ridge. "Look here. They will brag for days about killing our brothers! We are going to exact the cost of those brags."

"How?" Plenty Coups asked. "You said we must conserve bullets until the situation at our camp is resolved. And we are running out of gun cotton to hurl on them."

"Buck, we have an ample supply of primer caps and black powder. We are going to turn a favorite Cheyenne trick against their white masters. We are going to make their famous exploding arrows—the same arrows Touch the Sky used to defeat us in the Sans Arcs. Watch. It is simple."

Sis-ki-dee's copper brassards gleamed in the light as he worked. First, he used a length of buffalo sinew to tie one of the primer caps to an arrow point. Then he poured black powder from his flask into a little rawhide pouch and tied that around the cap.

"They fail about half the time," he said. "So have the men make a generous supply of them. We are going to launch them as one man, and you will see how we will make them pay. But this is only the bloody diversion. We are going to attack!"

Plenty Coups stared at him. "Attack? Contrary

Warrior, do you mean to go below and rush their camp?"

Sis-ki-dee threw back his head and roared his insane laugh. "Would you place a woman on the other side of camp if you meant to top her? You fool, how else can we attack them? Stop gaping and listen. They think they are safe. They have shaken us with the big-thundering gun. They won't expect an attack. We are going to rain exploding arrows in on them. Then while they are distracted with the fires, we will swarm on them. Make your thoughts bloody, buck, and nothing else!"

"Shh," Kristen said, trying to hush a crying child. "It's all right now, Mattie. Things are quiet outside now. It's all right, sweet love. Shush now."

Kristen rocked the little four-year-old in her lap. Other children too had taken shelter with their schoolmarm, a result of this most recent spate of fires. Now Kristen's house, one of the safest in camp, was crowded with wounded men and morose children.

Woman Dress, exhausted like everyone else, tended to the wounded miners as best she could. In the corner, hunched and deeply depressed, sat poor Sarah Blackford. Her mother Tilly lay dead, cruelly murdered, and so far they had not even been able to give her a proper Christian burial.

Justin McKinney, as plucky as his dad, stood guard near the front door with a shotgun under one arm. Some of the other older boys were armed too. Enough miners had been killed or wounded by now that they faced a very nasty prospect. Either the oldest boys would have to stand in for men, or this whole camp was doomed.

There was the noise of approaching feet from outside, and Justin brought his scattergun quickly up to the ready.

"Hello, the house," Caleb called out, knowing the nervous boys were armed and probably jumpy with fright. "Friends approaching. Lower your hammers!"

Kristen heaved a sigh of relief when Caleb and Tom, both exhausted and powder blackened but otherwise unharmed, entered the crowded room. Tom met her eyes and they exchanged a long look, then a smile. But his expression turned to a deeply worried frown as he surveyed the room with its grim and unhappy occupants.

"I'm hungry," Mattie wailed.

Kristen could barely hold back tears of frustration and rage. Mattie's mother and father were both missing and presumed dead. As for feeding all these hungry children, not to mention the men who were fighting this hard battle, she was helpless. The last of her flour and bacon had disappeared quickly, and even the coffee was gone.

"How does it look?" she asked Tom, who shook his head. Riley was not good at sugarcoating the truth, nor did he want to upset this woman whom he was falling in love with.

"They're quiet for now," he said. "Which worries me. They've got something else planned. I feel it in my bones. We've got the worst of the fires out now, but the men are dead on their feet with exhaustion. One more hard attack, and I don't know how long we can hold out."

Tom spoke low so none of the wounded or the

older kids would hear him. He glanced at Sarah, alone in her corner.

"She spoken to anyone yet?" he asked, pity clear in his tone.

Kristen bit her lip to keep from crying outright. She shook her head. "The poor thing is still in total shock. She doesn't understand it. Why would anyone kill her mother? And how will any of us explain it?"

"We won't," Tom said. "It's a scar that'll never heal. She'll carry it for life if she survives this."

He met Kristen's eyes again. "I just hope to God Matthew can get up to that camp in time and make enough catarumpus to pull them off us. If not—"

He broke off, unwilling to say what Kristen already knew without the words being spoken.

The four braves, two Kiowas and two Comanches, held counsel in a tight group at the top of the front slope of Wendigo Mountain. Below them, about halfway down, a huge belt of mist circled the mountain like a sash. Actually it was steam released by the underground springs, then trapped by wind currents. In the dim moonlight, they had just watched a lone rider come out of the steam and head for the top. They could not make him out clearly in the moonlight.

"It is Big Tree," said Sioux Killer, one of the Comanches. "Light is gleaming from his medal and the silver conchos on his saddle."

His companions were Sun Road, Bull Hump, and Scalp Cane. Good fighters all, they had been selected to protect the camp while the main body was dealing misery to the miners. The rest breathed easier at Sioux Killer's report and lowered their weapons.

"Something is on the spit," Scalp Cane said. "Big Tree is pushing his mount hard."

Soon enough their leader was within hearing distance, his tired mount blowing foam. "Look lively, brothers! Three Cheyenne bucks are on their way up to beard the lion in his den. Only the lion is going to rip their meat from their limbs."

Big Tree reached the camp, swung down, threw his bridle, and let one of his lickspittles lead the buckskin to the water trough that was kept filled from one of the underground streams.

"Are they fools?" Bull Hump scoffed, searching the slope below. "We can pick them off from here easier than lice from a blanket."

"We can pick them off easy enough," Big Tree said. "But not from here—from the back of camp. They are coming up the cliffs."

This evoked two chief emotions from the sentries: anticipation because this should be some lively sport and a rugged determination because each of them recalled what happened the last time they had let Cheyennes reach the summit of those cliffs.

"Is one of them the tall Bear Caller?" Scalp Cane asked.

When Big Tree nodded, the rest exchanged apprehensive glances in the moonlight. Big Tree mocked them with a sudden burst of laughter.

"Look at the squaw men on the feather edge of panic at the mere mention of his name! Follow me, bold warriors, and I will put the strength back into your limbs! Poke your fear into your parfleches. I tell you that he is still far down and will never make it. We are going to make sure of that right now."

Big Tree led them past the wickiups and lodges and storehouses to the rim of the steep cliffs on the backside of the mountain. "Start rolling boulders to the edge. Make many piles about a double arm's length apart so that we have the entire cliff covered. They are still below the steam; so we will not spot them. Nor is there much light down there even when they break through. But we will not have to see them to cause them the worst trouble in the world."

Indeed, Touch the Sky and his companions faced enough bad trouble as it was. The climbing was a bit easier now as hand- and footholds were more plentiful. But Little Horse had lost much blood, even though his wound was now well bound. There were times when, despite his heroic efforts, his companions were forced to carry his weight along with their own.

But worst of all, Touch the Sky realized, their enemy now knew they were coming up. The element of surprise had been ruined. They had only so much room to maneuver; so getting over that rim up above was going to prove a bloody piece of work, if it was even possible.

But it must be done! They had not come this far only to show the white feather and climb down. Look at Little Horse, Touch the Sky told himself—weak from blood loss, but carrying the fight forward anyway as he had always done. For he too knew the grim truth. Either they ruined that camp and thus cut off their enemy's supply line, or nothing would stop the formidable Renegade Nation.

These marauders had murdered Spotted Tail, leader of the Bow Strings. They had murdered Chief Gray Thunder. And now they meant to kill Chief River of Winds. Slowly, inexorably, they were chipping away at the rock of Cheyenne leadership and stability. Not just the white miners and their families were in peril. The Powder River Cheyennes were next.

So Touch the Sky fought on. His arms trembled with weariness. The three warriors inched closer toward the belt of steam. Once again, the nimble young brave covered a smooth expanse of cliff while his companions hung on for dear life and waited for the rope. Touch the Sky's eyes met Little Horse's. The plucky brave showed the great strain of his wound and lost blood.

"This is a better place to die than in your tipi!" Touch the Sky shouted down to him above the sound of raging wind. "But this is not a good night for dying! Death has another day reserved for you, brother. Your shaman feels it in his bones!"

Touch the Sky rarely invoked his status as a shaman, but doing so gave special credence to his words. Seeming to take heart, Little Horse renewed his efforts against the gray slate of the cliff face.

Touch the Sky reached a tiny ledge the width of perhaps three fingers. He hauled himself up, hugged the stone face, and again snubbed the rope around a rock spur. He knotted it and had just tossed it down to his companions when disaster struck.

Even as Touch the Sky looked up to gauge their distance from the roiling belt of steam, massive gray shapes came hurtling out of it. The deadly cascade livened the air all around them, and then a huge, solid boulder struck Touch the Sky hard on the forehead and tore him loose from his hold. For a moment, he almost recovered, with his hands and feet scrabbling for a grip. But he had been hit hard and his reactions were slowed. A solid ball of ice replaced his stomach when he began hurtling toward the deadly points of the basalt turrets far below.

Chapter Eleven

Sis-ki-dee could not make out the contours of mountain peaks in the darkness, only their shadowy mass. But he stared in the direction of the Wendigo Mountain camp, visualizing those cliffs. He had climbed them once himself—down only; and he had emerged from an emergency escape tunnel that opened on the cliff. Rather than face down Touch the Sky, he chose those cliffs.

His men worked all around him in the darkness, preparing the exploding arrows. Sis-ki-dee had heard nothing from the direction of Wendigo Mountain. That silence bothered him.

True it was, four stout bucks were guarding the camp. And Big Tree was even more trustworthy as a fighter. Still, this Touch the Sky grew meaner and more wily as his desperation increased. Sis-ki-dee had been gone to the south country when the Cheyenne's woman and child were kidnapped by Hiram Steele. But the widows left wailing after that particular mistake convinced Steele never to try it again.

And if his cunning foe reached that camp, Siski-dee knew that his five fine ponies were dust behind him. So was his cache of fine white man's tobacco and coffee, not to mention his handguns and other personal effects. Such a loss would destroy not only the Renegade Nation's ability to wage war; it would leave him and Big Tree as poor as their most dissolute braves.

So he knew his present plan was best. Never mind waiting for Touch the Sky to counter this strike. They must win with what supplies they had and return to their camp. With a victory, they could massacre the men below and ransom the women and children to the Comancheros. That would add to their riches. At least they could then afford to replace their goods if Touch the Sky's reckless plan worked.

"Contrary Warrior," Plenty Coups called out from a group of braves working in the light from the pit. "The arrows are ready."

"Stout buck! Divide them equally among all the men. Then line up at close intervals along the ridge. Don't worry about that thunder gun. You are not going to be on that ridge long enough to end up like our comrades. No one launches an arrow until my command."

"What targets?" Plenty Coups asked. "Only the mining equipment?"

"No, I want them concentrated on the houses too. We want fires, plenty of them. But have ears, brother! No one fires on the house I showed you earlier—the one at the end of the camp road."

*   *   *

"Jesus, it's damn near four a.m.," Tom muttered. "They've been quiet for too long now. I wonder how Touch the Sky is doing?"

The children were mostly asleep now. Nonetheless, Kristen found time to admonish Tom. "Now see here, Captain Riley! You are in my bad books!"

Riley's exhaustion gave way for a moment to genuine surprise. He sat up straighter against the wall that supported him. He watched Kristen rolling bandages she had soaked in gentian.

"Your bad books? What have I done?"

"I realize you're a soldier and you're used to a . . . vivid vocabulary in the field. But please watch all the cursing around the children! They already swear like little troopers as a result of the miners. You needn't encourage it, sir."

Though he was thus roundly rebuked, Tom could not resist a smile. Even caught between a rock and a hard place, this pretty girl insisted on the rules of civilized society.

"Sure is hard to sleep with my back to this wall," Tom said. "Caleb over there has the right idea."

Kristen, who was also worrying about what Touch the Sky was up to, didn't need to look to know that Caleb over there was asleep on the floor with his head in Woman Dress's lap.

"Hmph!" she said, glad Tom couldn't see her blush in the dark. "There's a pillow on the Boston rocker."

"Faith Gillycuddy is asleep on it. You wouldn't want me to wake her up, would you?"

"Well," Kristen said, "long as I have to sit and

108

do this anyway, I suppose it wouldn't hurt if you—"

Sarah, only half asleep, screamed at the sudden loud impacts all around them followed by popping explosions. Caleb shot up and clawed for his gun. Tom, halfway across to lie in his lady's lap, spun on his heel and raced toward the door.

"Damn!" he said. "What the hell are they doing now?"

Tom held the door slanted open enough that Kristen could see out into the camp street and beyond. Bright clusters of orange sparks seemed to leap off the houses. Some of them caused bad fires immediately as the little explosions spewed chunks of flaming wood everywhere, starting more fires—especially on the vulnerable shake roofs.

"C'mon, Caleb!" Tom roared above the din of terrified children. "Let's get to that Parrot gun before they burn this camp down around us!"

Little Horse and Two Twists, like their comrade, had been caught flush with surprise when those boulders suddenly showered down out of the band of mist above them. Touch the Sky was perhaps a double arm's length above them. The two of them were roughly side by side below him. Two Twists waited for the rope to be tossed down so he could assist Little Horse to the next ledge, where they might rest a moment.

Hurtling rocks barely missed both of them, but brushed by so close they could feel the breeze from them. Then before either of them could even blink, Touch the Sky flew past them. Little Horse's right arm speared out and managed to

109

grab Touch the Sky by an ankle; Two Twists' left hand shot out and barely gripped his comrade's red sash.

"Hold on, brother!" Two Twists roared out to Little Horse. "I only just have a handful."

"I have plenty," Little Horse said in a horribly strained voice. The plucky brave normally had the strength of a young burro. But much of that legendary strength had drained out with his blood. "Too much, buck! I cannot hold him much longer!"

"Try! He dropped the rope too," Two Twists said, "but it is tied above. Hold him just a bit while I see if I can get it tied around him."

However, this was far easier to say than to do. Two Twists had a reasonably good position, with his feet wedged into a fissure in the rock. But one hand had to hold Touch the Sky while he desperately tried to snare that rope with the other. Howling winds buffeted them and made his task harder, especially by blowing the rope just beyond his grasp.

"Touch the Sky!" Little Horse shouted. "Can you hear us?"

Their friend was ominously still, and they could see a gash opened to the bone where that rock had smashed into him.

"*Ipewa!*" Two Twists cried in Cheyenne when his fingers seized that errant rope. "Good!"

"Work fast," Little Horse urged him, desperation spiking his voice. "I am losing him, Two Twists!"

His face pinched with urgency, Two Twists managed to loop the dangling rope around his comrade and fix a knot on it just as Little Horse let go because he had to to save himself from falling. Unfortunately, there were still perhaps four feet of slack in the rope, which made a hard, fast snap as it tightened and Touch the Sky slammed into the granite facade of the cliff.

And thus things stood. The three of them, two exhausted and resting, the third unconscious, brought to a halt on that bare gray and hostile immensity of stone. Although Touch the Sky was safe for the moment, his companions did not even know if he lived.

The attack with those horrible arrows, Kristen quickly realized, had not lasted long. Clearly the savages up above had no intention of providing another target for the artillery gun. But though the actual attack was over quicker than a bad dream, the results had become a nightmare that wouldn't go away. Nearly half the houses were on fire, and the screams of frightened women and children drowned out the crackling flames.

Kristen and Woman Dress were under strict orders to remain in the house. But Kristen could not obey those orders, not with other women outside forming a bucket brigade despite the potential danger of a massed enfilade fire from above. A huge cistern at the back of camp collected rain water and snow runoff. Now a line snaked forward from it, and the desperate residents fought to save their homes and possessions.

Kristen asked Woman Dress to stay with the children and wounded; then she ran outside to assist the effort. She joined the far end, toward the direction of the mine itself. The Riley boys held their usual post at the Parrot artillery rifle. But both men, she could see in the eerie, bright orange glow of fires, scowled with frustration. The Indians had struck and then quickly retreated, leaving them nothing to draw a bead on.

Dakota Boggs's house, just to Kristen's left, was aflame, but still salvageable. She accepted bucket after heavy bucket, passing them on to the last woman in line, who doused the flames over and over. They were just beginning to make some headway when a hideous shriek, rivaling all the devils loosed from hell, assaulted Kristen's ears.

Startled, she glanced toward the entrance at the front of camp. A score or more of garishly painted savages, wielding every conceivable type of weapon, boiled up the slope, the kill cry distorting their faces. They fired their first volley, and Kristen heard a man scream as a bullet found him. But the savages had not yet spotted the Rileys under that limestone shelf. Even as the renegades poured deeper into camp, the last three ten-pound rockets whooshed in among them.

Too awed to take cover or scream, Kristen watched as powerful blasts literally blew redskins toward the heavens. Tom aimed with deadly skill, and the Parrot slowed the charge considerably. But an ugly leader she recognized as Sis-ki-dee himself rallied the last group of Indians coming up the slope.

Tom and Caleb's fighting fury was unbelievable. What they did next, Kristen realized later, saved the camp. A few miners had been all but routed by the Indian's massed charge. Bellowing commands in a voice louder than any plebe popping off at West Point, Tom organized and rallied them.

"Full front face!" he screamed to a ragged squad on his left. "Full front face and fire!"

Both Riley brothers deserted the gun, which was useless now. They ripped their sidearms out of their holsters and entered the melee at point-blank range. The other miners, watching Tom and Caleb rear up like grizzlies, were inspired to quell their retreat and join the fray in hand-to-hand fighting.

Kristen's life on the frontier had ever been perilous. But never had she witnessed a battle like this. It was awful, utterly terrifying, and yet it held her spellbound. Tom Riley looked like one of the berserkers she had read about in history books. His pistol empty, he used it as a club to smash at the invading horde.

Then, abruptly, a scream was torn from Kristen when a renegade shot Tom in the stomach and he folded to the ground. But at least Sis-ki-dee had decided this price was too heavy for the pleasure of exterminating these whites. Kristen saw him and his braves retreat down the slope even as she rushed forward to see if Tom Riley still belonged to the land of the living.

Touch the Sky dangled helpless on the feather edge of death as his mind played cat and mouse with awareness.

Brother! Brother, can you hear?

Yes, he wanted to say, tried to say. But could he really hear, or was it just a dream voice, part of his vision in the Black Hills? Memory flexed a muscle, time suddenly shifted, and he was back on Massacre Bluff where the white eyes held Honey Eater and Little Bear.

Shaman! Can you hear?

113

None of it held. Memory succeeded memory like geese flying in formation. Now he heard the voice of Old Knobby, the former hostler at the feed stable in Bighorn Falls: *The Injun figgers he belongs to the land. The white man figgers the land belongs to him. They ain't meant to live together.*

The melodic voice of Kristen Steele: *It scares me, all the enemies you've earned, all sworn to kill you.*

The hateful voice of Hiram, her father: *Now I've finally got this red son of a bitch pinned in the dirt. Let me see him squirm a little before I step on him.*

And now other, more familiar voices, even nearer: *Brother! Wake to the living world!*

Touch the Sky's eyes eased open.

"Brother!" Two Twists bellowed again above the piercing howl of the wind. "Can you hear me?"

"Pipe down, jay. I hear you," Touch the Sky said weakly. "Your shouts are like kicks to the head."

Thunder exploded, a rain squall slapped at them, and ghostly tines of lightning shot down from the sky.

"I will kick your head," Little Horse promised him gamely, "if we survive this unholy lump of misery. When I climb behind you, buck, I take my life in my hands! You almost flicked both of us off too. With a name like Touch the Sky, you'd best live up to it."

"Listen to All Behind Him," Two Twists scoffed, his voice implying that they were up against nothing more than a day in their camp. "That arrow should have hit you where you sit. You never would have felt it."

Touch the Sky was bruised and battered, but he could not resist a grin. His friends didn't fool him. Their brave banter was proof that now, more than ever, they were up against it. The code of the warrior was clear, and his band never deviated. Bear pain in silence; meet death with defiance.

"Bucks!" he shouted above the din of rough weather. "They are not done with us yet. Look sharp. Not only do we have to get up the rest of this cliff. We have to get over it. Now let's get it done. And if we cannot, then let us show them how well a Cheyenne can die!"

Chapter Twelve

"Those boulders made things lively for them," Big Tree said. "Count upon it. Those three noble red men will soon regret their rash impulse to beard the lion in his den."

The last of the rocks had been rolled over the cliff. The weather had cleared up, and a huge raft of clouds had been blown away from the moon. Now Big Tree's battle scars stood out in the moonlight as he scoured the camp, hatching more misery for the hapless Cheyenne interlopers. His four minions surrounded him.

Scalp Cane stared downward. "Very little light makes it down there. If they have climbed out of the steam yet, I cannot see them."

Big Tree gauged the time by judging the height of the dawn star in the east. "They will be up here soon. They will have to be. They know they will never stand a chance if they let Sister Sun catch them on that cliff face."

"A chance?" Sioux Killer gave out a harsh bark of laughter. "Quohada, light or dark, how can they have a chance of getting up here? Only think on this thing. I can almost toss a stone from one end of this cliff's rim to the other. If they go too far left, they will never get over that huge pile of rimrock. Go too far right, they encounter traprock shelves that would stop a mountain goat, let along two-footed men."

"I have ears," Bull Hump said. "The five of us can cover this rim secure in the knowledge that we have clear shots at trapped men who can hardly fire back while climbing for their lives."

"Clearly," Sun Road said. "Either they have been killed already by Big Tree's arrows and our rocks, or they have wisely climbed down."

"Listen to me," Big Tree told them severely. "You are good men—men to ride the river with, bucks! But false pride is dangerous where this Touch the Sky is involved. What kills a normal man only makes him more dangerous. Yes, our position is excellent here. But I do not think the Noble Red Man will give up his quest. And I agree that they can hardly clear that cliff while we are here. But I have no intention of hunkering down and biding my time until they appear to do battle. We are not done sporting with them!"

He pointed across camp to a spot where a wagon sheet had been staked out to cover several casks. They had been stolen from a whiteskin pack train passing through the Little Bighorn country. They contained chemicals long familiar to the Southwest tribes—the chemicals used to

117

Judd Cole

make white man's Greek Fire or gun cotton. Big Tree did not know how to pronounce the whiteskin names painted on these casks: niter, sulfur, and naptha. But he knew that the last of the three was highly inflammable by itself.

"Bull Hump and Sioux Killer," he ordered. "Go get that casket with the yellow signs on it. You, Sun Road and Scalp Cane," he added, pointing to a long wooden watering trough they had fashioned for the horses by splitting and hollowing a tree much as they might for a dugout. "Carry that to the edge of the cliff."

His comrades grinned and nodded, seeing which way the wind set. But Big Tree exhorted them, "Have ears, brothers! That exploding water will blaze at a moment's touch from a burning coal. We pour it into the trough, ignite it, and dump it over. Repeat this perhaps four or five times, and we can cover the entire length of the cliff. Hurry, bucks! The Cheyennes call this Wendigo Mountain. Now let us remind them why."

"Oh, merciful lord, he's lost so much blood," Kristen Steele muttered.

The pretty schoolteacher caught her lower lip between her teeth as she unbuttoned Tom Riley's military tunic to expose the ugly blue-black swelling where the bullet had pierced his stomach. The bleeding had finally slowed, but not before Tom passed out from blood loss.

"Belly shot," Woman Dress said sadly, shaking her head. Both women knew it was far better, if one had to be shot, to catch a bullet in the rib cage than in the stomach. Gut shots bled internally, and in a land where doctors were usually far off, that meant slow death.

118

"If this siege ends soon enough," Kristen mused out loud as she bathed the wound with a camphor-soaked cloth, "we can get him to Register Cliffs. Even without the train. We can use a buckboard. But it has to end soon."

Woman Dress looked worried at these words. Caleb was outside fighting fires with the rest of the able-bodied men. But she feared he would insist on trying to get his brother to help whether those Indians were gone or not.

"Maybe so better not go," she said in her halting, confused English.

Kristen let her head drop for a moment and massaged both her tired eyeballs with her fingers. How exhausted and spirit broken she felt! The children had finally cried themselves into a fitful sleep, and soon the sun would crest the mountains. What a night it had been! Tom lay dying, and what was Matthew's fate? If he hadn't gained the peak of that nearby mountain, they were all doomed here.

All of it was just so unfair! Kristen, forced to flee from her father's wrath like an antelope before a prairie fire; Tom, caught between the corrupt Indian Ring back in Washington and a sense of duty that forced him to fight secretly for his so-called Indian enemies; and Matthew, trapped between two worlds bent on his utter destruction. Hot tears welled up behind her eyes, but she fought them down. She would be of no use to anyone if she let herself break down.

Kristen went into the little slope-off kitchen and pumped up some fresh water. As she reached for the basin, however, her skin suddenly turned cold and grained with fear.

She glanced at the boarded-up window, thinking of the erosion gully that led down from the ridge above. But it was so steep at its beginning. And besides, why would any of the renegades pick on this house of all houses?

She was exhausted, she reminded herself. And nerve frazzled. She had to go take care of Tom Riley because until he got some help she was all that stood between him and death.

Sis-ki-dee unlooped his rope from the sapling, having finished the steepest part of his descent. From here, it was easy going to the back of the house. He paused behind the boarded-up window to listen. He heard men snoring and a child's cough. A sudden, metallic squealing made him flinch. Then he realized it was just one of the women pumping up some water. Sis-ki-dee reminded himself that some of the wounded might be able to fire at him. So he must work fast.

Moving silently, his moccasined feet feeling carefully to avoid dried sticks that might snap, he worked his way around the east wall of the wooden lodge. Cautiously Sis-ki-dee poked his head around to look into the main street. The sight gratified him. Although some buildings still smoked at this end of camp, most of the fires were concentrated farther down, and so were the men fighting them. A defensive line of riflemen, he could see in the ruddy glow of flames, guarded the entrance to camp.

As usual, he had timed things well. But like all battle leaders who had survived on these perilous plains, Sis-ki-dee knew that speed and surprise were essential. His blood sang in his veins, and if at all possible, he meant to take the white beauty outside and shame her in the dirt. But if he was discovered before he could get her mouth covered and drag her outside and around to the blind side of the lodge, then he would at least kill her on the spot.

No, she was not the proud Cheyenne beauty Touch the Sky had married. But the murder of this sun-haired woman would leave the Noble Red Man grieving for many moons. Perhaps, Sis-ki-dee thought with a sudden spurt of inspiration, he could even send him her scalp by a runner!

He checked the street again in the last of the night's dim blackness. Then Sis-ki-dee eased around the corner of the lodge, ducked under a window, and reached the split-slab door around front. He pushed against it. It resisted, but not before easing open an inch. It was only held by a latch string inside.

He checked the street once again, hugging the front of the house. Then, brass earrings glinting in the moonlight, he slid the bone-handled knife from his sheath. It was a mere heartbeat's work to slice through the rawhide thong holding the door. Sis-ki-dee pushed the door open a foot and peered inside.

He saw her immediately, bent over someone—Riley! He recognized the blue kersey tunic. She was wiping Riley's forehead with a damp cloth. The wounded lay here and there, interspersed with sleeping children.

Kristen Steele was absorbed in watching Riley and never thought to glance toward the door. Sis-ki-dee rose from his crouch and eased inside. Her beauty, seen close up in soft lantern light, made him pause for just a few blinks in his fast charge. Just long enough for the young girl sleeping in the rocking chair to wake up and scream loud enough to wake snakes.

Sis-ki-dee cursed. The rest happened faster than a digger could shoot an ox. Kristen Steele glanced up, started to scream, then took on a fighting scowl Sis-ki-dee could only call a war face.

Her right hand shot down to the officer's side and came back up holding his Colt Third Model Dragoon—or trying to anyway. This was one of the heaviest Colts known, the steel of its case-hardened frame weighted even more with a metal back strap.

Even as she lifted it, Sis-ki-dee saw the muzzle waver, then plunge. She fired, the sound deafening in this close lodge, and a big chunk of floor kicked up in front of him. He was only a few steps away now, closing fast, and he laughed outright at her comical attempt to kill him.

Then came a sudden shriek as unnerving as the kill cry of a Mexican lancer. Sis-ki-dee glanced right just in time to see the Crow Indian squaw lift her calico dress and slide a thin knife from her stocking. Her throw was not exactly grace-full, but a moment later he felt fangs rip into his right shoulder as the knife caught him just above his protective brassards.

He roared, as much in anger as in pain. But by now Kristen Steel had better control of that Colt Dragoon. Sis-ki-dee wrenched the knife from his shoulder and leapt for the door even as the gun exploded behind him.

"When we come out of this steam," Touch the Sky told his companions, "all three of us are going to pause for a moment and see how the wind sets. It has been hard to this point, brothers. Even now blood runs in my eyes, and it feels as if I have been mule kicked in the skull. Little Horse has lost so much blood he looks like a whiteskin. Only double braid here has not suffered a wound yet, and I fear his time is coming."

"I may skip the wound this time," Two Twists boasted between grunts of strain as he hoisted himself up. "I may skip it and go right to my death!"

The three Cheyennes had nearly passed through the belt of escaping steam that circled the entire mountain. Although half the climb still remained, it was the easy half—plenty of hand- and footholds. Unfortunately, Touch the Sky reminded himself, those delays caused by arrows and rocks had wasted valuable time.

"Never mind dying, buck," he told Two Twists as his companions came up beside him to counsel. "Not until I'm done with you. Now have ears, both of you. It is lighter than I thought. They will not be able to spot us just yet as we emerge. But I will guess they will have enough light to draw beads on us while we are still half this last distance down."

"So what?" Little Horse said. "It means that somehow we must cover the last distance while also firing at them to keep them respectful. It is possible to launch arrows from here on up by planting your feet good."

"It is," Touch the Sky said. "It is also possible to stand up in a canoe on the Snake River, but only a fool does it."

Both Little Horse and Two Twists exchanged a puzzled frown. Then Two Twists said, "Are you hinting, shaman, that we should go back down?"

"Go ask your mother for a dug! I will leave hints to the old squaws in their gossip circle. I will say it bold. With luck, we will neither go back down nor climb this cliff the rest of the way."

"Somehow," Two Twists assured Little Horse, "our comrade has found peyote growing up here and gnawed on it too long."

But Little Horse had finally seized his friend's meaning by the tail. "You mean the secret cave! The one Sis-ki-dee used to escape when we came up here to get our Medicine Arrows back."

"I mean just that, yes, and nothing else. Only think. We know he has one. He and Big Tree would never camp anywhere that had only one road in or out. We also know he got away from us somehow when we were in those caverns above us. They are not deep tunnels. One of them comes out somewhere up there. It has to."

They had begun moving upward again, and they cleared the swirling steam cloud even as Touch the Sky spoke. All three braves, thinking of that hidden cave mouth, stared upward—just in time to watch a roaring wall of deadly fire come hurtling down at them!

Chapter Thirteen

At first, time and place became confused. As that sheet of flame hurled down toward them, Touch the Sky was sure he was back on the prairie, caught in a grassfire. But the moment of stunned immobility passed in a blink, and the will to live instinctively asserted itself.

Just to Touch the Sky's left was a slight protrusion where the rock had buckled. Little Horse was already under it. Touch the Sky grabbed Two Twists and by sheer dint of will and muscle pulled him as he crowded in close to Little Horse.

"Press tight against the cliff!" Touch the Sky shouted. "Pretend it is your mother's breast!"

But speech was impossible as the roaring, air-borne inferno engulfed them. That protrusion just above them was their only defense. It served as a sort of dam, channeling this lethal flow slightly outward from the face of the cliff. All three Cheyennes grimaced with maddening pain as the passing heat seared them. A few drops of flaming naptha clung to their skin, the pain worse than a thousand fire ants biting them at once. But the fiery juggernaut dropped past them, turning the mist below to hissing steam. They held their positions, burned and shaken but afraid to move just yet. Several more times a wide line of fire flowed down, each time tracking along a different part of the cliff.

"They are sweeping the cliff for us," Touch the Sky called out.

Two Twists finally found his voice. "Brother, what manner of white man's devil is that?"

Touch the Sky shook his head, casting another worried glance topside. "Does it matter what name it goes by? Arrow Keeper always said that if it chops wood you may call it an ax. Whatever it is, it will surely kill us if we are caught in it. All the more reason to find that cave entrance."

"That and Sister Sun," Little Horse threw in, nodding toward the east. A band of sky over the plains was turning rose colored just atop the horizon.

"The burning water seems to have stopped for now," Touch the Sky said. "It is risky to break cover, brothers. But I fear greater danger if we hide here any longer. Fan out. Two Twists, climb up through that black lava rock and watch for openings. Little Horse, do the same through that belt of banded rock just overhead. I will search the rest of the cliff. And remember that whoever has been trying so cleverly to kill us may be waiting in the cave. So if you find the cave, signal by hand!"

* * *

"Brothers," Sioux Killer boasted, "if they survived that they are not mortal warriors. We did not miss any part of the front of the cliff. Shall we dump more, Quohada?"

Big Tree shook his head. "Save the rest. Sis-ki-dee and I have a bloody campaign planned for it once we have taken the mining camp. As for their death, believe it when we stack their bones and not before. More than once they have turned up from the dead after we have given a victory dance to celebrate killing them."

"Quohada," Sun Road scoffed, "the Bear Caller has salted your tail too often and turned you into a nervous old Ponca. Only think. You emptied a quiver full of arrows and got blood for the effort. We loosed half a mountain of rocks down on them and followed it with murderous fire."

"We have," Big Tree said. "Enough danger and death to wipe out a Pawnee camp. But have you forgotten what he did to us down in Bighorn Falls when we had his white parents surrounded? How many of our comrades may we no longer mention because Touch the Sky sent them under unclean? I say it again, and this place hears me. Only when I have taken a bite out of his warm heart will I pronounce him dead!"

"Big Tree speaks straight words," Bull Hump said. "But if they are coming, they will have to clear this rim. And already I can see the sun's glow on the horizon. The tall one will need all his shaman's tricks to elude our shots this time."

"Shaman's tricks," Sioux Killer said, "or a secret way up."

That chance remark suddenly sent ice into Big Tree's veins. A secret way up! What if Touch the Sky knew about the cave? Back at the front of

this camp was a huge cave that all the men knew
about. It was periodically used as a den by local
mountain lions. What the men didn't know, and
he and Sis-ki-dee did, was that a smaller maze of
tunnels spun off from this central cave. And one
of them ended at the cliff. It was just a tiny opening, barely large enough for a man and disguised
well in black lava rock at the extreme left edge of
the cliff face.

Touch the Sky would never spot the cave if he
didn't know about it. But what if he did? He had
chased Sis-ki-dee through those tunnels, but that
was long before Big Tree and his braves came
north. Big Tree didn't know if Touch the Sky had
guessed about it or not.

Big Tree couldn't take the chance. Nor could
he, with only four braves against Touch the Sky
and his men, dare to split this small force. Yet
there was no other way to guard both this cliff
and that cave.

"Scalp Cane," he said. "You stay here and
guard carefully. If you see them, fire your rifle to
summon us. The rest of you, come with me. I
have thought of something. There may by chance
be a cave down on that cliff—one that connects
with the cave up here."

Big Tree led his men toward the cave. An old
wagon box sat in the middle of camp, the legacy
of a raid on a whiteskin pack train. He had his
men drag it along with them to the cave. Set up
on end, it neatly covered the opening.

"Good." Big Tree picked up a huge boulder—
one twice the size of any his companions could
manage—and thumped it down in front of the
wagon box. "Pile on the rocks, bucks! We must
be sure they will not be able to come out this way.

If they are still alive, the only way into this camp will be by that cliff."

Touch the Sky, battling fierce winds and hard climbing, scoured his section of the cliff. But no opening bigger than his fist penetrated the solid rock. He glanced to his left just in time to see Two Twists desperately signaling to him and Little Horse.

"I found it, brother," he whispered when his comrade joined him. The youth pointed. Sure enough, the opening was small and, in the black lava rock, almost impossible to see from more than a few feet away. Truly, it was not much bigger than the smoke hole of a lodge. But a man could get through it, Touch the Sky realized. And three men would get through it.

But who was harassing them? If it was Sis-ki-dee, they were very well marked for death. He would have a trap waiting.

"You hog all the sport," Little Horse said when Touch the Sky started to worm his way into the entrance. "Let me go first."

Touch the Sky ignored him—and the fearful pounding of his own heart—and wiggled farther into the hole. His body dropped through onto cold, damp stone. He moved in farther and his companions came in after him.

"If they mean to spring a death trap on us," Touch the Sky said quietly, "it will come later. Keep both eyes to the sides. I have never been in this tunnel, but closer to their camp there is a confusing maze of them. I only hope I can recall the way out."

Normally, Two Twists or Little Horse would have added some bold comment and scoffed at death. But what they were doing right now, crawling trapped in an enclosed space, was contrary to their nature as Indians. Even from their tipis they could always see the sky. In here, all was cold, dark, and cramped like a premature grave.

Soon they had other troubles. The small tunnel gradually widened, allowing them to stoop, then stand upright. But it connected with other tunnels, and each one they followed seemed to double back around on itself. Finally, however, they entered one vaulted chamber and Touch the Sky felt the back of his neck tingle. His shaman sense was telling him he had been here before.

"Here," he said in the darkness. "We are close to the way out."

"How can that be?" Little Horse said doubtfully. "I remember that cave you mean. It had a tall, narrow entrance that let much light pass. All is darkness here, yet outside the new sun is coming up by now."

"They have blocked the entrance," Touch the Sky said with certain dread. "Search the walls! If they have blocked us in, there is nothing else for it. We will have to find our way out and finish our climb in daylight."

"Here!" Little Horse called out after a little time had elapsed in desperate searching. "I feel wood. And I can feel a faint breeze."

"This is the entrance," Touch the Sky said. "And they have blocked it. Brothers, I know you are tired, especially you, Little Horse. That wound in your leg would have a lesser man groaning in his robes. But now we must set our shoulders to this wood and see if we can budge it."

The warrior did not expect the job to be easy. However, the moment he strained against that wood Touch the Sky knew it was blocked from behind by plenty of weight.

"It does not even begin to budge," he said, fighting off a wave of dizzy nausea. The effort took its toll after that long climb up and the injury to his head.

"We can burn it," the resolute Little Horse said. "Burn the wood, I mean, and see if we can move what is behind it?"

"They may see the smoke," Two Twists said.

"So what?" Little Horse said. "They may see our smoke, and they will see us coming up that cliff. Would you rather be told you might die or you will die?"

"Now All Behind Him has become a logician," Two Twists said.

"Yes," Touch the Sky said, breaking out his flint and steel. "And a persuasive one, at that."

All of them always carried crumbled bark in their parfleches and legging sashes for tinder. Touch the Sky sprinkled some at the base of the dry, weathered wood. Then he struck flint to steel, throwing a few sparks downward. Soon the bark caught, and he carefully fanned it to life. The wood slowly caught fire, sending a brighter and brighter orange glow to light up the cavern.

"It is an old wagon box," Touch the Sky said, recognizing the forged iron bands around it.

All three braves were forced to back up as the flames and smoke increased. Any moment, Touch the Sky expected shouts from outside. But soon the flaming wood crumbled inward under the weight of boulders, and a little window of dull light appeared at the top of the heap.

"We have some work ahead, Cheyennes," Touch the Sky said. "But they should all be gathered near that cliff at the rear of camp. If we work quickly, we are free of this place and in their camp! Hands to the work, bucks!"

Once again, Touch the Sky's days among the white men stood them in good stead, and he organized a quick system for clearing the heap. Little Horse was the weakest of the trio, and the least able to move around agilely. So Touch the Sky put him at the end of the line and Two Twists in the middle. Then the tall brave climbed onto the heap and began rolling the boulders down to Two Twists. He heaved them back to Little Horse, who rolled them aside and out of the way.

The window grew until it was big enough to let him squeeze through. Touch the Sky's companions followed him out, Two Twists and Touch the Sky helping Little Horse.

The sun was up now, and all of them were drenched with sweat from their efforts. For some time, they crouched in the heap of rocks and kept a wary eye on the deserted camp while they regained a little of their strength.

"I can see no one," Little Horse said.

"Nor I," Touch the Sky said. "But they are all up at the cliff. We can't see it from here until we go through the camp."

Go through the camp they did only a few moments later. Cautiously, in single file, they crossed from tree to rock. They passed through the deserted lodges, past the hut storehouses, and up the rest of the mountain until the rim of the cliff eased into view. Using hand signals, Touch the Sky called his companions up to his side.

"Look," he whispered. "Maiyun lined them up for us."

He pointed off to the north. Four figures were crouched at various points along the rim of the cliff. Each one stared intently down, rifle or bow to hand.

"Are there more?" Little Horse wondered.

"If so, where? We have come through the camp."

Even as they spoke, all three warriors notched arrows into their bows and pulled the buffalo-sinew strings taut.

"Today is a good day to die!" Touch the Sky shouted out in Sioux, knowing the renegades understood it.

The three Cheyennes waited until their startled foes had spun around, bringing their weapons up as they did. Fletched arrows hissed through the morning mist, and cries of pain followed as the expert archers skewered their targets in their vitals. Two dropped dead above, and two more fell back off the cliff, one of them screaming so hideously he made the hair on Touch the Sky's nape tingle.

The tall warrior thrust his bow in the air and shouted, "Hi-ya, hii-ya!" His brothers joined his victory shout.

But even as their exalted voices split the mountain stillness, Touch the Sky spotted something in the corner of one eye. He glanced quickly to the left toward the front slope that led up Wendigo Mountain. He was just in time to see a lone figure leap out from behind a rock and tear off down the slope. Then he realized their terrible mistake. The massive size of that figure meant it could be only one Indian: the Comanche war leader Big Tree.

133

Chapter Fourteen

"Burn it, brothers," Touch the Sky said to his companions. "Every lodge, every cache, every weapon except those you claim as trophies. Make piles and heap them high. Once the flames are licking, use robes and wagon sheets to make plenty of smoke. We want the rest at the mining camp to see and know their siege is ended. Their enemies have lost their base of supplies!"

Little Horse, limping and tired, but also eager to begin the destruction, glanced at his comrade. He and Two Twists had not seen the figure leap from behind a rock.

"Shaman," Little Horse said. "Whenever you place your hand on the haft of your knife like that, bloody business is close at hand. What do you know that we do not?"

"You called me shaman, buck, and you said

right. Listen to the birds, and they will tell you what I have in mind."

"What birds?" Two Twists demanded. "There are no birds up here."

"There are two puzzled jays," Touch the Sky said. "Named All Behind Him and Double Braid. Just set to work, brothers. I have a piece of work out on the slope. I have just seen a wild longhorn. You know how the wild ones are. The Mexicans call them *ladinos*, the sly ones. Sometimes they seem to run away, but they hide and then attack."

"Longhorns?" Two Twists asked. "The cows down to the south in the land of sagebrush and greasewood? Why would one be in the mountains?"

Little Horse, who knew Touch the Sky's indirect ways better than most, said, "Never mind, tadpole. Swim down to the camp and let us set to work."

"Kill the ponies," Touch the Sky said as he headed toward the slope. "But lead out three for us. I like that grullo and that blood with the white forelegs. And find me a good weapon for the ride back."

"Don't let those longhorns gore you," Little Horse called out behind him.

Touch the Sky had no desire to tangle with Big Tree right now. He was far from good fighting fettle, and a man who locked horns with that superb Comanche warrior had best be in top form or expect to feed worms.

But Little Horse had immediately understood what the less experienced Two Twists had not. Touch the Sky's reference to the famous man-killing cattle in Texas did indeed fit Big Tree. It

135

was one of his favorite tricks to be seen fleeing a trouble spot; then he would double back and score surprise kills while his quarry celebrated or rested. Touch the Sky had no plans to chase Big Tree down the mountain. But he would at least cover that slope while his friends destroyed the camp. Otherwise they were at risk from the back-shooting Comanche.

Even as he braced his leg muscles for the downward slope, Touch the Sky heard an eerie, hideous trumpeting noise behind him. He realized that his friends had wisely decided to start with the horses since the destruction and fire would spook them. That noise was air rushing through the slits in their windpipes. It saddened him greatly. These wild mustangs were fine mountain stock descended from the best Spanish breeds. Like the best Indians, the best mustangs had freedom in their blood and resisted conquering by the hair-face invaders.

But the warrior chastised himself for such distracting thoughts. He recalled one of the first lessons in survival that Arrow Keeper had taught him. At moments of danger, a warrior must stop the inner flow of words called thoughts and attend only to the language of the senses.

The sun was well up, but still cut off from this south face of Wendigo Mountain. As Touch the Sky let his gaze cross the entire slope, he studied and read the shadows. Then he turned sideways and studied it with his peripheral vision. Sometimes that could reveal movements that direct vision could not.

Touch the Sky moved a little way down and searched behind the bigger rocks as he did. Behind him, a sudden burst of sustained gunfire

made him wince until he realized it was ammo
stores burning. He hoped his friends got out of
the way in time. Already, it sounded like a full
battle.

Good! Let the noise shake the very sky, for they
had been forced to endure the sounds of battle
from the mining camp. Now let Sis-ki-dee hear
some of the same.

Touch the Sky took a few more steps, paused,
then heard a faint metallic click. A less experienced man might have stopped to puzzle that
sound out. But the Cheyenne recognized it without needing a moment's reflection.

Blood surged into his face, and Touch the Sky
tucked and rolled just as the gun went off. There
was a sharp tug at his rawhide shirt when the
bullet passed through the folds under the armpit.
But he got to a stack of rocks and hunkered behind them.

Big Tree's harsh laughter barked. "Bear Caller!
You would be dead right now if only I followed
Sis-ki-dee's advice. He always carries his rifle
cocked with a bullet in the chamber. I leave my
hammer on an empty chamber. I will not ruin
another shot at you by cocking a weapon and
warning you!"

"I cannot wish the fault undone, Quohada. And
neither will you undo the damage my comrades
are doing to your camp and horses. Hear it?
Smell the burning stink of it? The Renegade Nation will live like lowly, filthy Diggers, grubbing
for roots and sleeping in holes. And while you do,
thank three Northern Cheyennes who made all
of it possible for you."

These words were shot straight. Big Tree and
Sis-ki-dee were able to play the big Indians, in

137

part, because of the wealth they had amassed over the years, booty seized in countless raids. Now that sign of their status was going up in flames along with everything else. Touch the Sky could tell, from Big Tree's wooden tone, that his goading words just now were barbs landed in vitals.

"Boast, White Man Runs Him! Your masters in the mining camp are not out of trouble yet. And by now, Sis-ki-dee has left his seed in your paleface cow. As for you and your lickspittles up in my camp—you have a long ride down, and I will be playing with you!"

Keeping a careful eye on his back trail, Touch the Sky returned to the camp, or rather, the blazing inferno that had been the camp. The destruction was complete. And after that harrowing climb up the cliffs, it was a gratifying victory. But Big Tree would be as good as his word. They were in for a dangerous ride down.

"Count upon it, brothers," Touch the Sky assured his companions as they hurried to set out. "It isn't just a hard ride ahead for us. We have destroyed their camp and thus their ability to hold siege. But Big Tree, puffed up with his pride, will want one last chance to destroy the miners. By now Caleb and Tom and Liam, if even alive, will need all the fighters they can count."

Little Horse had cut out a fine grullo, a solid blue-black mare, for Touch the Sky. The Cheyenne often rode off-color breeds, but had discovered that the solid hues were most durable. Touch the Sky salvaged a hackamore and blanket from the ruins of the camp.

"Here," Two Twists said, handing his tall comrade a Colt Model 1861 musket. "They have left no repeaters in camp, but this came from Big Tree's lodge. A fine weapon, and very similar to the one you had when our tribe captured you. The one Wolf Who Hunts Smiling stole and never returned."

Touch the Sky nodded and lay the .58-caliber weapon over the grullo's withers at the ready. Little Horse had selected a dun, Two Twists an ugly little paint with powerful haunches. Both braves had found rifles too, Little Horse a brass-frame Henry and Two Twists a North & Savage revolving percussion rifle.

"The trail is wide until we reach the belt of steam," Touch the Sky said. "We'll ride abreast. Once we hit that belt, throw caution to the winds and goad your steeds! Trust in their instincts to place their feet on that trail and ride full out. Big Tree must not have a slow-moving target in that mist."

His companions nodded. The ponies, muscle cramped from the small corral, were eager for exercise and difficult to control, especially with new riders on their backs. These mounts were hardly tamed, and that wildness almost made Touch the Sky wish they had bits in their mouths. Sometimes the white man's cruel ways made sense.

They had barely gained the slope before a gunshot from a hidden position reminded them of their danger. Two Twists's paint crow hopped wildly, and he fought her down only with hard effort.

Another shot rang out a few moments later; this one hummed past Touch the Sky's ears. But Little Horse thought he caught a glimpse of muzzle flash. He fired down the trail at a little niche in the solid wall of rock to their left. Sure enough, Big Tree flashed into view for a second as he moved to another position.

"Brothers," Two Twists said, "a thing troubles me. Why would Big Tree have left camp without a mount?"

"We frightened him out too fast," Little Horse boasted.

But Touch the Sky shook his head. "Big Tree is a Comanche. He would take his chances in camp before he would flee without a horse. They have ponies cached in several grazing spots closer to the bottom. Big Tree knows all the shortcuts and defiles and cutbanks. He can get down there on foot almost as fast as we can mounted."

"And this way," Little Horse said, seeing his friend was right, "he can make our lives a hurting place from hiding."

"Eyes to the side," Touch the Sky said again.

However, Little Horse's shot had sent Big Tree ahead for now, and they reached the edge of the wide steam belt without further incident. Now, using hand signals to minimize the warning to Big Tree, Touch the Sky formed them in a single file. The path here, as it entered the blinding steam, not only steepened its grade but narrowed. It would make for a perfect ambush.

"Remember," he said in a low tone. "Let the horses feel your heels! Ride close to their necks with weapon to hand. Two Twists, stop pulling your pony's nose up. Let it sniff the ground. That is how they feel danger. They will obey better if you let them feel the ground."

They nodded, and he kicked the grullo's stout-muscled flanks hard. The mare had been waiting for a chance to run, but this blinding mist held her to a frustrating trot. Touch the Sky rode first, followed by Two Twists and then Little Horse.

Once again Big Tree proved the Comanche skill at terror and menace. Mocking shouts, seeming to emanate from all around them, soon rang out in the swirling white confusion.

"Bear Caller! By now Sis-ki-dee has topped your white woman and cropped her ears to mark his victory! And I had your Honey Eater when she was our prisoner at Blanco Canyon. She resisted at first, but when she experienced a true man, she cried out and begged me for more!"

Touch the Sky tried to locate the source of the voice. But wet air confused sounds, and it came from any direction he cocked an ear toward.

"Woman Face! You have a fine son. I mean to hold him by the ankles and brain him against a tree. I will dry his skin and use it for a parfleche."

Another shot rang out, the bullet splatting from rock to rock as it ricocheted. Touch the Sky's horse began sidestepping dangerously close to the right side of the trail, where it dropped off precipitously into nothingness. Touch the Sky leaned far forward and bit her savagely on the left ear. The ancient trick worked. She gentled enough for him to muscle her back onto the trail.

But the next shot brought more trouble. Touch the Sky heard a heavy crash behind him as Two Twists's paint dropped dead. He whirled just in time to see the youth barely lift his leg out of the way in time to avoid being trapped.

"Two Twists!" he shouted, extending a hand. Two Twists gathered up his weapons and swung up behind his comrade. Touch the Sky was about to urge his mount forward again when something caught his eye up ahead. Barely visible in a cleft between two rocks was a man in hiding.

The tall warrior reached one arm out to stop Little Horse as he too rode up. Touch the Sky nodded silently toward the form. His two friends saw it and nodded back.

Keeping his voice to a whisper, Touch the Sky said, "Big Tree has finally found his own grave, bucks. He does not realize the mist is thicker up here than down there. We can see him, but he cannot spot us yet. Wait here and draw a bead on him. I am sneaking around behind the rocks. When you hear my musket speak its piece, take your shot also. We have three chances to finally kill him."

Touch the Sky chewed off the paper end of a cartridge that contained the powder and ball. He poured the powder down the barrel of his Colt, then pushed the bullet in with his thumb. He drew the ramrod from its mounts and pushed the projectile down the barrel. He pulled back the hammer and seated a percussion cap on the nib beneath it.

His weapon ready, he eased off the trail and behind the piles of scree that had been cleared away long ago when the renegades made this path. Touch the Sky fought down the frantic pounding of his heart. This was not just any ordinary kill, but an attempt on Big Tree. Many good men had gone under trying to kill the Red Raider of the Southwest country.

The mist swirled and eddied all around him. He moved from rock to rock, praying to Maiyun that he would not make any telltale noise. And soon, with the Day Maker's help, he had taken up an excellent position above the crouching figure.

Against an honorable warrior, Touch the Sky would never have accepted a surprise kill. A brave who upheld the warrior code deserved to face his enemy in a fair fight, a fair test of wills and courage. But this was a murderer of women and children, a back-shooting criminal lower than the bloody Utes who massacred whiteskin wagon trains in the mountains. Killing this red criminal was a duty, not an honor.

The figure held still. Touch the Sky drew a bead dead center, then eased his finger inside the trigger guard and took up the slack. The musket bucked in his hands, and he had the intense satisfaction of seeing the figure below suddenly flinch as the bullet caught him.

Two more shots rang out to Touch the Sky's left as his companions opened fire. Both shots scored hits, and Touch the Sky cried out with eager gladness.

But his joy died when he reached that niche and discovered the cruel hoax Big Tree had played on them. The man they had just stalked and shot was a buckskin shirt stuffed with grass. Even as they stared at each other, Big Tree's mocking voice called out below them. "Good shooting, Cheyennes! You have just shot *odjib*, the thing of smoke! Will you scalp him too and tell the brothers in your lodge how you counted coup on twigs and grass? Mighty red men!"

His mocking laughter was followed by the fast thudding of unshod hooves.

"You were right, brother," Little Horse told Touch the Sky. "He had a pony cached."

Touch the Sky nodded, already hurrying back

to his own mount. "Big Tree has foxed us again. And now you do not need your shaman to tell you what comes next. They mean to mount a final strike on the miners and, if possible, before we get there to interfere. Now we ride, brothers. The battle of all battles is coming."

Chapter Fifteen

"You mocked me," Sis-ki-dee said bitterly. "Threw it back in my face that I failed to kill him at Bloody Bones Canyon. This time, you swore, it would get done because Big Tree himself, the Big Indian, would take care of it. Now you crawl whipped from our ruined camp, swallowing back your own prideful words. Admit it, Quohada! He is the better man."

Sis-ki-dee and Big Tree stood well back from the long ridge overlooking the paleface camp below. Even now, with their shadows slanting eastward in the declining sun, they could still see black smoke boiling from Wendigo Mountain as the last of their camp smoldered.

Rage sparked in Big Tree's dark eyes. "I admit nothing of the kind, Contrary Warrior. And if you are a better man than Big Tree, bridge the gap. I am for you."

For a few tense moments, the two braves, both bitter with frustration, squared off. Menace seemed to mark the very air between them. Then, abrupt as a thunder clap, Sis-ki-dee tossed back his head and roared with laughter. A bloody cloth was wrapped around his right arm just above the brassard—the legacy of that Crow squaw's accurate knife-throwing arm.

"Look at us, Quohada! Ready to gut each other, and over what? It is not just you he made a fool of. Once again, he goads all three of us: you, me, and Wolf Who Hunts Smiling. But do you not see it? If we kill each other, the tall one wins. Who will be left to kill him?"

For a long time, Big Tree, still smarting from his failure, brooded. But slowly, he began to nod his head. "Spoken straight-arrow, buck. He wins indeed if we two clash. Wolf Who Hunts Smiling is right. We must cross our lances as one until that tall one is sent over. Then we can turn to the task of killing each other."

"He has ruined us," Sis-ki-dee said, glancing again at that roiling smoke. "My ponies and weapons and liquor are all smoke now."

"And all my fine battle trophies," Big Tree added. "Along with all our food and stock."

"Our men know what happened, Quohada. And they blame us! I have heard them complaining among themselves. They too have lost everything—the results of many winters of raiding and hard work."

"Good. That anger," Big Tree said, "can work in our favor. You know that the fight here is almost over?"

Sis-ki-dee nodded. "Indeed. That is why those three brazen warriors climbed those cliffs."

"As you say. We must give it one more bloody effort. How is our ammunition?"

"Plenty of arrows. Not so many bullets. We are low on pig lead."

"Enough," Big Tree asked, "to sustain one more charge?"

Sis-ki-dee nodded, the brass rings in his ears glinted in the setting sun.

"Good," Big Tree said. "Those Cheyennes must still ride back into the camp below. I was well ahead of them. That means we have one more chance at killing them when they ride in. But kill them or not, we must make preparations to strike one last time."

"Buck, we tried once while you were on Wendigo Mountain. We almost breached their entrance. But it was a bloody business, and many good braves did not come back. Now we are too few, I fear, to mount an attack in force, especially if Touch the Sky and his minions return first."

Big Tree pondered all this. "If only we had another way down. Some other way that would let us split our force. A diversionary group could hit the entrance slope again. When all the miners rushed there to defend it, we could slip the second group down."

"There is a second way down," Sis-ki-dee said. "It is steep at some places and requires a rope. But once past those places, it is easy going. It is a runoff gully that ends among the houses."

"I have ears for this! A man can swat one mosquito, but two can drive him crazy. We will talk to the men first and get them breathing fire for this kill. They are angry at us, but we must direct that anger at our enemies."

"Sis-ki-dee!" Plenty Coups yelled from a position to their left, overlooking the entrance slope. "Here come riders on our ponies!"

"They are returning," Big Tree said. "Grab your rifle, Contrary Warrior. Now is our chance!"

Sis-ki-dee pulled his North & Savage from its sheath and hurried to the south end of the ridge. Now they could spot three riders on two horses boldly racing toward the slope.

"Plenty Coups!" Sis-ki-dee called out. "Roan Bear, Hawk Nose, Battle Road!" he shouted, naming the best shots among the men. "Now is our chance, bucks! Let daylight into their souls!"

"It is working, brother," Little Horse said, peering out from his hiding place just below the slope. "They are killing us now!"

"Good," Touch the Sky said. "Run for it, brothers! Keep to the right. They are all watching the horses on the other side."

How fitting, Touch the Sky told himself, that his enemies were falling for the same trick Big Tree had just played on them. Those Indians on those ponies were buckskin suits stuffed with grass, complete with feathered headdresses. From so high above, they looked real enough.

"Caleb!" Touch the Sky shouted out in English. "Caleb, Tom, Liam! We're coming in on foot. Hold your fire."

"Now!" he told his comrades, and all three made a break for it.

They fanned out wide of each other, all of them running a zigzag pattern. Little Horse, with his wounded leg, had a rough time of it, but he lumbered along as best he could. At first, as they skirted boulders and clumps of bushes, the going was easy. Their enemy were distracted and did not notice them. Then a shout from above changed all that.

All of a sudden, Touch the Sky heard bullets and arrows chunking into the ground and trees all around them. They were almost safe, and he could see Caleb and Liam desperately running from cover to move a line of stakes out of the way. But Little Horse was falling farther and farther back. Blood loss had finally caught up to him and sapped his last reserves of strength.

"Brother!" Touch the Sky yelled to Two Twists. "Catch!"

Still on the run, Touch the Sky flipped one end of one of his ropes to Two Twists. The youth caught it. Working with perfect coordination, they flipped the rope back and behind the flagging Little Horse's back. Both braves pulled the rope taut, propelling Little Horse with it. When his feet were finally swept out from under him, the game warrior merely grabbed the rope and let his comrades pull him in the last few dozen yards. It was a rough finish, giving him a few bruises and cuts. But he was safe.

Caleb loosed a whoop. "By God, no Texas wranglers could fancy rope better than that. Am I glad to see you boys. We knew you got their camp when we seen all that smoke. And just in time. It's coming down to the nut cutting around here. Signs show they're going to try at least one last strike."

Caleb, Liam, Touch the Sky, and his comrades had all taken quick shelter behind a stack of shoring timbers.

Touch the Sky glanced around. "Where's Tom?"

Caleb's elated expression sank into a worried

frown. "Tom's stove up. Bad. Caught a slug in the gut. Kristen and Woman Dress are doing what they can for him. But if we don't get him to a doctor pretty damn quick, he's a goner. We almost lost Kristen too. But Woman Dress ran a knife into Sis-ki-dee's arm."

"Kristen's all right?" Touch the Sky demanded sharply.

Caleb looked startled. "Yeah, she's all right. The thing of it is, nobody knows how he got down here. Kristen thinks maybe behind her house. There's an erosion ditch there, but I think it looks too steep farther up."

"Judging from those dead renegades we saw coming in," Touch the Sky said grimly, "Tom made them pay for the privilege of shooting him."

"Tom saved our bacon while you were gone," Liam said. "I never saw a man stay so frosty under fire! He rallied all of us and kept those bastards from taking this camp. Damn savage Indians—uh, sorry, Touch the Sky. Didn't mean you and your bunch."

"Brother," Little Horse complained between chews. He and Two Twists were both working away on strips of pemmican since there had been little time to eat lately. "Will you talk hair-face talk all night? What are you saying?"

Touch the Sky told them Tom Riley was shot and perhaps dying. This news sobered his friends and settled them from the elation of their latest victory over the renegades. In general they despised the *Mah-ish-ta-shee-da*, the Yellow Eyes, as their tribe called white men, because the first whites they ever saw were mountain men with severe jaundice. But Tom Riley, like Touch the

Sky's boyhood friend Corey Robinson, spoke one way to the red man. Whites who did not speak from both sides of their mouths were rare. And Tom Riley had placed his life in danger to save their tribe. In fact, he was doing so now. Once this camp fell, Powder River would be next.

"Either Tom will soon get to a doctor," Touch the Sky said, "or he will be dead along with the rest of us. Our mission to Wendigo Mountain has cut short this siege. But as you said, they'll try one last strike."

The words of Honey Eater's father, Chief Yellow Bear, came back to him now from his vision at Medicine Lake: *When all seems lost, become your enemy!*

"What are your plans for the defense?" Touch the Sky asked Caleb.

"Well, I figure they'll try an attack in force. But then again, that didn't work last time. And now they've got fewer braves to do it. So to tell you the honest-to-God truth, Touch the Sky, I don't rightly know. With Big Tree and Sis-ki-dee, how the hell can you?"

"You can't," Touch the Sky said.

"So I'm mainly calling it by good ol' gut hunches. What you red sons call medicine."

Caleb pointed toward the stakes. "This bunch is different from you Northern Plains warriors. You boys like to hunker round the fires at night if you can. This bunch loves to strike after dark, and that's when I figure they'll play their ace. You agree?"

Touch the Sky shook his head. "No, I don't. Everything you're saying is smart and logical and the best possible deduction based on their past

151

behavior. But they know you know that. Understand me?"

Caleb looked confused, but some light began to glimmer in his eyes. "So you're saying they'll bluff me?"

The Cheyenne nodded. "I think so. I'd say the attack will come anytime now, but before dark. And as for the attack in force, it didn't work last time. I predict they'll fake it, but try something else."

Caleb glanced at the main line of his men, dispersed along the entrance to camp. "You suggesting the men be moved?"

"First of all, are those explosive charges still buried out there?"

"They need to be checked," Caleb said. "They might have been disturbed during that last attack. We had no time to light the fuses then."

Touch the Sky nodded. "We'll check. Assuming the nitro packs are still in place, I'd leave you here in charge of lighting them and a light force up front. No more than five good shots to hold back the decoy group long enough for you to get the explosives lit. I'd include Little Horse if he can still stand. With that revolving-barrel shotgun of his, he can clear out a canyon."

"It's risky, buddy. Damned risky if you're wrong. If they storm us from the front again, I can't stop all of them with two explosions. Well, where would you put the main force of men?"

"Nowhere," Touch the Sky said.

Caleb looked like a man who had gone to bed in one country and woken up in another. "Nowhere? You want to spell that out plain?"

"Glad to. You give up white man's tactics for

once and fight like Indians. These are Indians attacking us, aren't they?"

Caleb was getting interested. "Hell, don't whack the cork now. What do you mean by fight like Indians? Whoop and use arrows?"

"Funny, paleface, real funny. No, I mean that for once quit thinking that all you can do is fort up and take one position. The main point here is that we don't know what they'll do this time, right?"

"Sure, but—"

"And since we don't know, we don't want your men pinned to one spot."

Caleb was catching on. "You mean, keep the main group as roving skirmishers, ready to hustle anywhere? Hell, yes! Like the Green Mountain Boys and Rogers' Rangers."

"I had the Apaches in mind," Touch the Sky said dryly, and Caleb grinned.

Both men looked around as Touch the Sky translated the main points for his comrades.

"They'll try to find another way in," Touch the Sky assured Caleb. "And they'll send at least a light force at the front. So we have to have a built-up position and skirmishers on the move. And just in case, we had better tell the people in the houses to arm themselves with what they have."

Caleb nodded, his face grim. "I've already got all the boys twelve and over out on guard. We've lost too many men."

"And you'll lose some more," Touch the Sky said. "Bear in mind, Caleb, that neither one of those bucks brooks humiliation. It's not just the defeats here. Their camp is a shambles. I know the ritual by now. Right now, those Kiowas and Comanche devils are getting nerved with liquor

153

and corn beer, the last they have thanks to us. This next strike is not going to be a strike for booty. It's bloodlust now, and a hard fight is coming."

Chapter Sixteen

Touch the Sky's predictions proved right. However, Big Tree and Sis-ki-dee added some cunning twists to their strategy, and fate intervened, ensuring a pitched battle whose outcome would hang in the balance until the last bloody charge.

Working quickly, Touch the Sky and Two Twists risked fire from above to verify that the nitroglycerin blocks were still in place, blasting caps and fuses attached. Touch the Sky recalled something Tom had mentioned about how sharp, concussive impacts—such as from a bullet—might also detonate them. On a hunch, he had Two Twists follow his example in exposing one corner of the blocks aboveground. Not enough to make them obvious, just enough to offer a bare target.

"None of them shot at us while we were exposed," Touch the Sky told Caleb when the two braves returned to the relative safety of the built-up area. "That troubles me."

Little Horse, under strict orders from his comrades, was lying on his sleeping robes, resting. But he had his shotgun and captured Henry rifle to hand.

"They are quiet now," Little Horse said after his friend switched to Cheyenne and repeated his remark, "only because they are busy preparing the attack."

"I've got the men distributed like you said," Caleb told Touch the Sky. He nodded toward the light force nearby. Five adults were backed up by an equal number of boys, Justin McKinney among them. "That's all we got defending the front. If the men are killed, the boys have strict orders to rush forward and fill in. The rest are in two skirmish groups farther back. I hope you're right, hombre."

"If I'm not," Touch the Sky said grimly, "we had better hope that those boys become men quick and that the skirmish groups can respond quick to plug the gap. You just make sure you live by those fuses. Those nitro blocks could be the key to dispersing the forward attackers. You got the timing down?"

"I think so, but that part'll be tricky. Tom said something about testing the fuse because the powder can dry out."

"Too late now," Touch the Sky said, glancing up at the ridge. "If they see us fooling around with it, we'll ruin the surprise. You can't quite see it from here, but we left the blocks exposed to gunfire from a little closer. Bullets will detonate them. Remember that in an emergency."

"An emergency?" Caleb muttered. "That's all we've had around here."

"Double braid," Touch the Sky said to Two Twists. "We are going to cut our horses out from the corral. Little Horse will be up here with the defending force at the entrance. You and I will watch how things develop and take the fight where it is needed."

Two Twists approved of this strategy. It was a fitting way for an Indian brave to fight, not hunkered down behind breastworks.

"Look!" Caleb pointed down the slope. A line of braves was descending the ridge by a narrow trail, streamered lances held high.

"Here comes the fight!" Touch the Sky called out in English, then Cheyenne. "One bullet, one enemy!"

"You might have called it right," Caleb said, counting the descending braves. "That ain't near half their force. But, dammit, it's still more than we can hold back if they all rush at once."

Soon, however, all discussion ended as the attacking renegades took up positions and began firing into the defenders.

"Hold your first shot!" Caleb roared out to his men. "They want to charge while most of us are reloading!"

As if sensing the presence of those nitro blocks, the attackers held back from a main charge in force. Touch the Sky could see Big Tree directing the attack from this end, which meant Sis-ki-dee and the rest were somewhere else. But where?

"Should I call some of the skirmishers up front?" Caleb bellowed out, his face set tight with worry.

"No," Touch the Sky said. "We can hold here."

But that was not at all clear to the defenders. Big Tree cleverly drew off their fire with several feints. Then, abruptly, a knot of perhaps ten renegades threw a line of stakes aside and rushed them.

Little Horse's shotgun roared, rock salt tearing faces to red smears. Touch the Sky emptied his Sharps and his captured musket, and Two Twists fired too. This sent the surviving renegades reeling back while Touch the Sky charged his weapons. But a tenacious Big Tree, realizing the defenders were reloading, sent another line of men almost immediately.

"Justin!" Caleb screamed, desperately thumbing rounds into his pistol. "All you boys, on the line and fire!"

The frightened but determined boys, several armed only with small-caliber squirrel guns, darted forward and discharged their weapons. Fear made their aim careless, but they bought a precious few seconds for the Cheyennes to grab their bows from their rope riggings. Still mounted, easy targets, they nonetheless unleashed a firestorm of deadly arrows.

This stopped the attack once again. But the victory was costly. Half of the defending line were dead or wounded; others were out of ammo. The boys moved up onto the main line of defense. But Touch the Sky feared they would not hold one more assault.

The momentary lull in this fight only drew attention to the abrupt explosion of battle noises behind them. Touch the Sky whirled around in his saddle and saw a score or more of braves pouring down that erosion gully behind Kristen's house. But this part of the plan he had anticipated brilliantly. Liam McKinney had formed the skirmish groups to meet them, and renegades were dropping like flies as they descended into a hail of lead.

No, it was this end of camp that stood in danger. More than he had allowed for. And now Touch the Sky could see that Big Tree had decided to unleash the final assault. Two Twists saw it too; so he dismounted, giving up the Indian style for the white man's as he forted up beside Little Horse. Touch the Sky's shaman sense, however, warned him not to follow suit. He must stay mounted, ready to move.

"Caleb!" he shouted desperately above the din of battle. "Here it comes! Light the fuses!"

A wall of lead slammed into them as the attackers hurtled forward. Caleb bent down, fumbling for a match; a moment later, Touch the Sky watched in horror as blood blossomed from his chest and he was slammed backward.

From where he sat, Touch the Sky was closer to the charges than he was to those fuses. And besides, enough time had been lost that the fuses might not burn quickly enough. There was only one hope. He had to get close enough to shoot those nitro blocks.

The warrior knew it meant sure death for his pony and probably for himself. But the determined Cheyenne tugged his hackamore hard left and kicked his palomino into motion. He charged into the very teeth of the oncoming renegades.

Now he risked being killed by his own side, especially those inexperienced boys behind him. He could hear Little Horse and Two Twists mocking their enemy with shouts. Closer still

Touch the Sky pounded, bullets whistling past his ears.

The main force of the attackers was rapidly drawing even with those nitro blocks. But a heartbeat later, Touch the Sky felt his pony crash beneath him as she caught a round in her lights.

The first renegades reached him. He had his lance to hand and skewered one; another felt the obsidian blade of his knife. But Touch the Sky refused to fire his recharged rifle and musket, each looped over a shoulder. A few more braves streamed past him, and the roaring Two Twists rose with knife in hand, leading the miners and the fired-up boys in desperate hand-to-hand combat. They were fighting like she-grizzes with cubs, but if many more of those attacking renegades got past Touch the Sky, he knew his friends were doomed.

The tall Cheyenne searched desperately for sight of one of the charges. When he found it, he shrugged his Sharps off his right shoulder. He needed to get a little closer, but death could find him at any moment if he waited. As the main body surged over that charge, he fired and missed!

So desperate he cursed in English, Touch the Sky shrugged the Colt musket off his left shoulder. Now, even if lucky, he could only set off one of those blocks. It would have to be enough, or the battle was all over.

Touch the Sky drew a tight bead, took in a long breath, and willed his muscles to relax as he took up the trigger slack. The musket kicked in his hands. Then there was a whip-cracking explosion like an ice flow breaking up, and the air was filled with flying rocks, dirt, and bloody chunks of Indians.

That explosion broke the back of the beast. The attack down the erosion gully had already failed, and the remainder of the renegades fled back up to the ridge. Liam's skirmishers set up a lusty cheer at the same time as the survivors up front, who watched Big Tree and his defeated men retreat in a rout.

" 'Earth to earth, ashes to ashes, dust to dust,' " said Levi Carruthers, a miner who had been a Methodist preacher back in St. Joe. " 'In sure and certain hope of the Ressurection unto eternal life.' "

Quietly, as the victims of the renegade siege were finally laid to a decent rest, Touch the Sky translated the solemn words for his curious friends. They both paid strict attention. Like most red men, they were in awe of all matters spiritual. It fascinated them when Touch the Sky explained that white men too believed in an afterlife for worthy warriors.

The three Cheyennes stood respectfully at the front of the gathering because the miners had insisted their heroic friends be prominently placed. Caleb and Tom were absent; they had both been rushed into Register Cliffs by buckboard as soon as the siege lifted. Though they were missed today for the burial of their friends, at least the news was good concerning their injuries. Tom had lost much blood, but he would recover. Caleb was in even better shape, and he should be back on the job shortly.

Meantime, things were up and running. The telegraph had been repaired, the tracks soon would be, and as soon as possible, Liam planned to get at least one shift working in the mine. Caleb had payroll to make, and it was time for these big galoots to start earning their breakfast again.

Kristen Steele, severely pretty in a black bombazine dress and a wide-brimmed hat, stood among the braves, her eyes glistening with tears as Tilly Blackford's pine coffin was lowered and the ropes were pulled out from under it.

"Brother," Two Twists said awkwardly to Touch the Sky, his voice low, "not one of these miners is a coward. But why are many of them crying like the women?"

"White man's customs permit it at funerals. It is not considered a loss of manhood. Whites believe that if grief is not expressed now it may hurt them more later."

Two Twists and Little Horse exchanged glances. This reasoning was curious, but contained a hard nugget of truth. Perhaps these hair faces knew something, after all.

The Cheyennes had waited instead of returning to their camp right away—waited to make sure the renegades were truly gone and waited so that Little Horse could recover his strength. The delay was not crucial. Touch the Sky had heard from a camp runner that Tangle Hair had performed his job admirably. Honey Eater and Little Bear were safe.

But the renegades were indeed gone. They had returned to their ruined camp to lick their wounds and nurse new grudges. No one was foolish enough to think them finished. However, it would be many moons before they could again seriously threaten anyone in these parts.

Nor, as Touch the Sky gazed around this gathering of mourners, could he forget what else that word bringer from camp had told him—a message from Wolf Who Hunts Smiling, who had obviously heard the news about the renegades' failure. "Blood will beget blood, Woman Face. We offered to share the spoils with you, but you refused. Now dig in for the fight."

Let it come, Touch the Sky thought grimly, looking at all these sad faces. He belonged to no clan, to no soldier society; and his enemies claimed he carried the stink that scared away the buffalo. But who among them could also say he feared any warrior?

Touch the Sky's eyes met those of his comrades, and no words were needed. All shared one thought: *The next fight is coming, and we have been promised a share in it.*

CHEYENNE

JUDD COLE

Cheyenne #19: Bloody Bones Canyon. Born the son of a great chieftain, raised by frontier settlers, Touch the Sky returns to protect his tribe. Only he can defend them from the renegades that threaten to take over the camp. But when his people need him most, the mighty warrior is forced by Cheyenne law to leave them to avenge a crime that defies all belief—the brutal slaughter of their beloved peace chief, Gray Thunder. Even Touch the Sky cannot fight two battles at once, and without his powerful magic his people will be doomed.

_4077-8 $3.99 US/$4.99 CAN

Cheyenne #11: Spirit Path. Trained as a shaman, Touch the Sky uses strong magic time and again to save the tribe. Still, the warrior is feared and distrusted as a spy for the white men who raised him. Then a rival accuses Touch the Sky of bad medicine, and if he can't prove the claim false, he'll come to a brutal end—and the Cheyenne will face utter destruction.

_3656-8 $3.99 US/$4.99 CAN

Dorchester Publishing Co., Inc.
65 Commerce Road
Stamford, CT 06902

Please add $1.75 for shipping and handling for the first book and $.50 for each book thereafter. NY, NYC, PA and CT residents, please add appropriate sales tax. No cash, stamps, or C.O.D.s. All orders shipped within 6 weeks via postal service book rate. Canadian orders require $2.00 extra postage and must be paid in U.S. dollars through a U.S. banking facility.

Name _____

Address _____

City _____ State _____ Zip _____

I have enclosed $_____ in payment for the checked book(s).

Payment <u>must</u> accompany all orders.☐ Please send a free catalog.

CHEYENNE

JUDD COLE

**Don't miss the adventures of Touch the Sky, as he
searches for a world he can call his own.**

Cheyenne #14: Death Camp. When his tribe is threatened
by an outbreak of deadly disease, Touch the Sky must race
against time and murderous foes. But soon, he realizes he
must either forsake his heritage and trust white man's
medicine—or prove his loyalty even as he watches his people
die.
___3800-5 $3.99 US/$4.99 CAN

Cheyenne #15: Renegade Nation. When Touch the Sky's
enemies join forces against all his people—both Indian and
white—they test his warrior and shaman skills to the limit.
If the fearless brave isn't strong enough, he will be powerless
to stop the utter annihilation of the two worlds he loves.
___3891-9 $3.99 US/$4.99 CAN

GORDON D. SHIRREFFS
Recipient of the Owen Wister
Lifetime Contribution Award

Now He is Legend. Ross Starkey is a loner, a drifter, a fighter who lives by his guns and rides wherever the money is—to range wars in the north, to revolutions south of the border, to any renegade who has the right price. Now Starkey wants out, and there is just one thing that stands in his way—a man they call the Tascosa Kid. Ross' only friend, his partner, and now his bitter enemy, the Tascosa Kid will keep Ross from hanging up his guns…even if it means killing him.

_4124-3 $3.99 US/$4.99 CAN

Bugles On the Prairie. In lawless towns from Santa Fe to Calaveras County, Ross Fletcher will need every ounce of courage and cunning he possesses to avenge the death of his brother, stop a deadly ambush, and rescue a beautiful woman held captive under the searing Arizona sun.
And in the same action-packed volume….
Rio Bravo. Somewhere beyond the Rio Bravo, two women are held hostage in the wilderness by an Apache chief who plans his master stroke against the white eyes. And when Lieutenant Niles Ord, U.S. Calvary, throws his frontier troop onto the bloody scales of battle, will he tip the balance toward victory—or go down fighting?

_4078-6(Two complete Westerns in one volume!)$4.99 US/$5.99 CAN

Dorchester Publishing Co., Inc.
65 Commerce Road
Stamford, CT 06902

Please add $1.75 for shipping and handling for the first book and $.50 for each book thereafter. NY, NYC, PA and CT residents, please add appropriate sales tax. No cash, stamps, or C.O.D.'s. All orders shipped within 6 weeks via postal service book rate. Canadian orders require $2.00 extra postage and must be paid in U.S. dollars through a U.S. banking facility.

Name _____

Address _____

City _____ State _____ Zip _____

I have enclosed $_____in payment for the checked book(s).
Payment must accompany all orders.☐ Please send a free catalog.

A mighty hunter, intrepid guide, and loyal soldier, Dan'l Boone faced savage beasts, vicious foes, and deadly elements—and conquered them all. These are his stories—adventures that made Boone a man and a foundering young country a great nation.

DAN'L BOONE: THE LOST WILDERNESS TALES #1:

THE LOST WILDERNESS TALES

DAN'L BOONE

DODGE TYLER

A RIVER RUN RED

The colonists call the stalwart settler Boone. The Shawnees call him Sheltowee. Then the French lead a raid that ends in the death of Boone's young cousin, and they learn to call Dan'l their enemy. Stalking his kinsman's killers through the untouched wilderness, Boone lives only for revenge. And even though the frontiersman is only one man against an entire army, he will not rest until he defeats his murderous foes—or he himself goes to meet his Maker.

_3947-8 $4.99 US/$6.99 CAN

 **Jake McMasters**

Follow the action-packed adventures of Clay Taggart, as he fights for revenge against soldiers, settlers, and savages.